Matt indicated the pin.
"You're a survivor, aren't you?"

"I am," Hannah said, always finding it easy to smile with the thrill that she was in remission now. "But I also lost my mother to breast cancer, like Autumn. So I know how much it hurts."

Matt tilted his head, curiosity at Autumn's awareness still evident on his face. "Well, for some reason, she was drawn to you."

Hannah felt flattered...and honored. She remembered her silent prayer, asking God to let her help this little girl. He'd undoubtedly granted her request. "Maybe because I'm meant to help her?"

That made him smile, and Hannah couldn't deny the impact that his smile had on her heart. He was so genuine, so honest and so concerned with his daughter.

"I know this will sound a little odd," Matt said, "but I think maybe you're right. Maybe the reason I picked this town, the reason Autumn and I are here is...because of you."

Books by Renee Andrews

Love Inspired

Her Valentine Family
Healing Autumn's Heart

RENEE ANDREWS

spends a lot of time in the gym. No, she isn't working out. Her husband, a former All-American gymnast, co-owns ACE Cheer Company, an all-star cheerleading company. She is thankful the talented kids at the gym don't have a problem when she brings her laptop and writes while they sweat. When she isn't writing, she's typically traveling with her husband, bragging about their two sons or spoiling their bulldog.

Renee is a kidney donor and actively supports organ donation. She welcomes prayer requests and loves to hear from readers! Write to her at Renee@ReneeAndrews.com or visit her website at www.reneeandrews.com. Check her out on Facebook and Twitter as well.

Healing
Autumn's Heart
Renee Andrews

Love Inspired

Recycling programs
for this product may
not exist in your area.

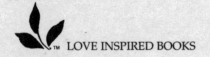

™ LOVE INSPIRED BOOKS

ISBN-13: 978-0-373-87701-0

HEALING AUTUMN'S HEART

Copyright © 2011 by Renee Andrews

All rights reserved. Except for use in any review, the reproduction
or utilization of this work in whole or in part in any form by any
electronic, mechanical or other means, now known or hereafter
invented, including xerography, photocopying and recording, or in
any information storage or retrieval system, is forbidden without
the written permission of the editorial office, Love Inspired Books,
233 Broadway, New York, NY 10279 U.S.A.

This is a work of fiction. Names, characters, places and incidents are
either the product of the author's imagination or are used fictitiously, and
any resemblance to actual persons, living or dead, business establishments,
events or locales is entirely coincidental.

This edition published by arrangement with Love Inspired Books.

® and TM are trademarks of Love Inspired Books, used under license.
Trademarks indicated with ® are registered in the United States Patent
and Trademark Office, the Canadian Trade Marks Office and in other
countries.

www.LoveInspiredBooks.com

Printed in U.S.A.

The Lord is good, a refuge in times of trouble.
He cares for those who trust in Him.
—*Nahum* 1:7

This novel is dedicated to my husband,
J.R. Zeringue, and my boys, Rene and Kaleb Zeringue.

"A happy family is but an earlier heaven."
—George Bernard Shaw

ACKNOWLEDGMENT

Special thanks to breast cancer survivor Doris Green
Zeringue, my wonderful sister-in-law,
for sharing her diary, her knowledge and her heart.
All mistakes are mine.

Chapter One

Matt Graham had to walk with a slight lean to hold Autumn's small hand as they exited Nelson's Variety Store. He'd hoped that the uniqueness of the old-fashioned five-and-dime with its soda jerk counter, malt machine and 1950s charm would appeal to his six-year-old daughter and maybe even result in a smile. Or, if he could be so lucky, more than a single word.

He glanced down and admired the shiny miniature black and white tiles displaying the store's name on the concrete in front of the building. The letters were block-style and reminded him of Autumn's homework from last night. Her first-grade class had been learning about a different letter of the alphabet each week since school started, and this week's letter was *E*. For each of the last four weeks, while she studied *A, B, C* and then *D,* he tried to bring her homework into their daily conversations, or rather *his* daily conversations, since most of their discussions were entirely one-sided. It was merely another attempt to converse with his daughter. So far, he hadn't had much success, but maybe this week would be different.

God, let me break through her wall somehow. And please, God, let it be soon.

Matt sighed, wondering why he still found himself praying at all. He supposed it was more habit than anything else. Because he'd prayed continuously two years ago, and it hadn't saved Rebecca.

He looked back at the tiles and hoped God had decided to give him a little help this week with his daughter. Heaven knew he needed all the help he could get.

"Look, Autumn, that says Nelson's. And it has an *E* right there—" he pointed to the letter "—just like the ones you were writing on your paper last night."

Her soft brown curls brushed against his arm as her head tilted to look at the tiles.

Matt paused, waited, hoped.

After a couple of beats, he prompted, "Maybe we could buy some tiles or blocks from the toy store and you could make your letters the way that they did to spell the name of their store. We could put them on the coffee table in the playroom or on the kitchen table, if you like." He smiled. "I think it'd be fun to make letters that way, don't you?"

Brown doe eyes, his precious Rebecca's eyes, looked back at him, and the sadness filling their depths pierced his soul.

Matt's heart squeezed tightly in his chest. She looked so much like her mother. He forced what he hoped was an encouraging smile. "What do you think? Does that sound fun?"

She blinked, looked back at the tiles and whispered, "Maybe."

Matt swallowed, nodded and started down the sidewalk toward Tiny Tots Treasure Box, the toy store located on the other side of the town square. He tried to feel positive about the fact that at least she held his hand. There was some form of connection left between them if she'd still do that, or that's what the last psychologist they visited in Atlanta had said. But Matt didn't want a "connection" with the one person he cared for more than any other.

He wanted a bond.

Moving to the tiny community of Claremont, Alabama, had been his last-ditch effort at making that happen. Away from Atlanta, away from his research, and away from the home that held way too many sad memories and not nearly enough happy ones.

The quaint country town nestled amid the foothills of Lookout Mountain had "friendly and inviting" written all over it, right down to the town square, where he'd brought Autumn today after school. But they'd been here two months and she was still trapped inside the protective cocoon she'd created when Rebecca died.

A six-year-old shouldn't know what it's like to lose her mommy. He sighed and realized that a thirty-year-old shouldn't know what it's like to lose his wife, especially when the one person who could have potentially saved her was…Matt.

They continued down the sidewalk, and Matt took in the town's charm, from the splashing tiered fountain that centered the square to the colorful planters filled with cascading flowers hanging from wrought iron lampposts along the street. Resident geese gathered near the fountain and squawked loudly as they awaited bits of bread from a gray-haired man sitting on a bench nearby.

Matt inhaled, and the air still held the faint scents of summer, but the gentle coolness of fall. Several couples window-shopped hand in hand, and Matt easily recalled when he and Rebecca would have done the same thing on a beautiful day like this, enjoying the comfortable weather of late September by spending the afternoon outside. They'd never lived in a small town since his research kept them in Atlanta, but she would have liked Claremont. She would have taken great pleasure in sharing this picturesque town square with Matt and Autumn. If Rebecca were here, she'd be laughing, no doubt. She had loved to laugh. He imagined her mocking the squawking geese and coaxing Autumn into doing the same.

Matt glanced at the geese, their black mouths stretching wide as they encouraged the old man to toss more bread, then he looked down at Autumn to see what she thought of the noisy birds. Her head was down, her attention focused on the sidewalk beneath her feet. Matt didn't even attempt to mimic the birds. It wouldn't come across the same way it would have if Rebecca did it, and it really wasn't the type of thing he'd ever done with his little girl. He was always the serious one and Mommy the funny one, until Rebecca became so sick that she stopped laughing at all. Matt tried to recall the last time he heard Autumn laugh.

He couldn't.

Obviously he'd have to settle for small steps toward connecting with his daughter. Today she held his hand. He supposed that would have to do.

A few people said hello as he and Autumn met them along the square. Matt made sure to nod, smile and return the greeting. He was the new doctor in town, after all, and even though he was still learning the families that were the backbone of Claremont, he realized that most of the small town knew who he was, which was evident when he and Autumn met an elderly woman standing outside of the square's barbershop.

"Well, hello, Dr. Graham. It's good to see you again," she said, then turned her attention away from Matt and to his daughter. "And how are you today, Autumn?"

Matt racked his brain but couldn't place the lady. She hadn't been in to his office, he was sure of that. He made a point of remembering each patient's name. *"Knowing someone's name lets them know you really care, not only about their health, but also about them as a person,"* Rebecca had often reminded him, and Matt had agreed. But even though this lady wasn't a patient, her face looked vaguely familiar.

"Are you having a good time with your dad?" the woman continued, and Matt realized she was waiting for some type of response from his daughter.

He gently squeezed Autumn's hand and hoped it was enough encouragement that she would say something. Anything.

Autumn nodded, and Matt figured he should be thankful that she responded in some manner. Even though school had only been in session for a month, her teacher had already called him in twice to discuss her lack of communication skills, and Matt had assured the lady that Autumn was still coping with losing her mom and that she'd be better soon.

He'd been telling himself the same thing for two years.

"How did you like the book you checked out this week?" the woman asked. "You got a Curious George one, didn't you?"

Autumn nodded, and Matt's mind clicked into gear with the memory of this woman—Mrs. Ivey, he now recalled—showing off Claremont Elementary's updated library at the school's orientation night.

"Her grandmother has been reading it to her each night before she goes to bed," Matt said, and smiled, picturing Maura sitting beside Autumn in the bed and telling her all about the adorable monkey and the man with a yellow hat.

Matt's mother-in-law had been grateful to him for asking her to move with them to Claremont. She'd wanted to be a part of her granddaughter's life and was more than happy to take care of Autumn each afternoon until Matt got home from work.

"Well, we have plenty of Curious George books in the library," Mrs. Ivey said, "so if you want, you can check out another one next week when your class has their library day. Okay?"

Another nod from Autumn, and Matt didn't miss the way Mrs. Ivey's mouth flattened at the solemn gesture and then the undeniable look of pity that she reflected toward his precious little girl.

Thankfully Mr. Ivey chose that moment to exit the barbershop and join his wife. Her attention taken off of Autumn, the librarian introduced her husband, told Autumn she would see her at school and then the couple continued down the street.

"She's a nice lady," Matt said. "And she even remembered which book you checked out. That's pretty special, don't you think?"

He took a few steps then heard Autumn whisper, "Yes."

Yes. One of four words he'd heard out of his daughter's mouth since Rebecca died. *Yes. No. Okay. Maybe.* Nothing more, nothing less.

Matt didn't know what else to do, didn't know what else to say. The disconnect between himself and his little girl, between *everyone* and his little girl, was so intense that he was starting to think it'd be easier for him to perform surgery blindfolded than to get her to open up, which was why he thought he was imagining things when she stopped walking, pointed to the toy store and said her first full sentence in two years.

Her words were softly spoken, so quiet that Matt couldn't make them all out at first. So he asked, "What, honey? What did you say?"

Autumn didn't answer, but her brown eyes widened, and she moved closer to the toy shop's window, where Matt now noticed a woman assembling a complex display of several miniature houses.

Apparently realizing that she had visitors, she finished placing a tiny barbershop pole outside one of the buildings then turned, looked at Matt and Autumn, and gave them a full smile.

Beautiful. The first word that came to mind at the image in the window. Her face radiated happiness, confidence, and a mesmerizing beauty that rendered Matt quite speechless. With dark eyes, high cheekbones and full lips, she had an exotic appeal, in spite of her traditional attire. She wore a pink T-shirt, cuffed blue jeans and sparkly silver ballet slippers. Her brown hair was short, with the edge of wispy curls barely touching her collar, and her bangs were pulled to the side and pinned back with a bright pink jeweled barrette. Still smiling, she motioned toward Autumn and crooked her finger, inviting them to come inside.

To Matt's shock, Autumn tugged on his hand, looked up at him and smiled. She *really* smiled. Then his dear little girl repeated the same words Matt thought she'd said earlier, only he heard them clearly this time.

"She's like Mommy."

Hannah Taylor felt like a kid in a candy store, or maybe a kid in a toy store, since that's exactly where her work had taken her for the past week. She had been over the moon when Mr. Feazell approved her window display for the Tiny Tots Treasure Box. Recreating Claremont's town square with dollhouses had definitely been one of her biggest challenges as a window dresser, but she'd risen to the occasion, and the toy shop's owner was thrilled with the interest the display was already getting from the community.

Plus, the fact that he'd sold six of his most elaborate dollhouse kits since she began the display last Monday didn't hurt his enthusiasm. And today, even though it was the middle of the week, the town square had been filled with people eager to enjoy this beautiful weather.

Naturally, they all window-shopped, which meant they all noticed Hannah's displays at each store.

She grinned. Who would have thought that she could make a career out of designing the windows in the Claremont square? No, she wasn't exactly using her interior design degree to its fullest potential, but she hadn't really gotten that degree for a job anyway. She'd gotten it because her mother had asked her to, and at that point in time, she'd have promised her mom anything. Anything at all. And she was designing, even if that meant decorating single windows instead of entire houses.

Hannah still had one more promise to keep for her mom, and she had no doubt that she would. Eventually. God had been too good to her to let that other part of her mother's last wish fall through the cracks. Besides, that had been one of her own dreams, too, that she would find the man God had made just for her and that they'd live a long, happy and hopefully healthy life together.

Please, God, let it be a healthy life.

She rocked back on her heels and eyed the town square coming to life before her in intricate dollhouse form. It was a bit difficult working on the houses at floor-level, but she'd placed the display low because she knew who her real audience was—the children of Claremont. There would be lots of kids at the First Friday celebration next week and they would undoubtedly be captivated by seeing the center of their town brought to life in the toy store's window.

Hannah still had a good deal to accomplish before the monthly festivities, but everything was coming together fairly well, and she truly believed that she'd make good on her promise to Mr. Feazell that his window would be one of the favorites at October's First Friday event.

Today she'd added Mr. Crowe's Barber Shop to the group of buildings already complete. Hannah knew his portion of the square was extra special to the locals. For the past sixty years, practically every little boy in Claremont got his first haircut in Mr. Crowe's chair.

Many of the retired men in town were actually younger than Mr. Crowe and remembered when the eighty-two-year-old first opened the shop way back in 1951. Back then they were excited about the swirling barber pole and the friendly young man who ran the place. Now they all hung out there for more than the customary cut, shave and hot towel that the sweet old man provided. They gathered there for the camaraderie, for the memories of days gone by and for a glimpse of the future, as the next generation brought their little guys in to crawl up on the big black chair, sit on the cracked leather booster seat and create a memory.

Hannah smiled, enjoying the fact that she could bring the town she loved to life in the display. Every store had a story, and she hoped that the exhibit encouraged some of the folks around town to share those stories.

That had been her goal, the primary selling point that she'd used when she convinced Mr. Feazell to go with the rather elaborate, detailed display. She'd told him that this wasn't merely an exhibit; it was a collaboration of Claremont memories. Hannah's life had taught her how important family and friends were, how important your hometown was, and how extremely important memories could be. This display brought all of that together.

She had recognized most of the people who'd stopped to view the scene today, which was to be expected, since Claremont was fairly small and most everyone knew everybody in town. In fact, merely a half hour ago, Mrs. Ivey, the librarian from the elementary school, stopped by with her husband. They'd come inside the toy store so they could get a better look at Hannah's interpretation of Mr. Crowe's shop. Mr. Ivey had marveled at the tiny black barber chair and laughed when he noticed the abundance of miniature newspapers and magazines scattered around the customer chairs. He'd been surprised to see that Hannah had even included a mini shaving brush with the barber tools on the counter and that it appeared to be covered in white foamy cream.

"Look at the window," Mrs. Ivey said, pointing.

Hannah had taken a fine-tipped paint brush and written Crowe's Barber Shop on the small rectangular window in bright white craft paint. She'd taken the time to walk down to the shop, copy the cursive style of the writing on the actual window and then mimic that font on her dollhouse replica. The little details were what made a scene special, and Hannah loved adding those unique tidbits to the display.

"Isn't it amazing that you can get that kind of detail in a dollhouse?" Mr. Ivey had said.

Hannah and Mr. Feazell, who made sure to visit with each person that came in to see the display, both agreed.

Mr. and Mrs. Ivey's admiration cemented the fact that the scene had the impact Hannah desired on folks that viewed the tiny town. In fact, the two of them recalled the day Mr. Crowe opened his barbershop sixty years ago, when they were merely dating teenagers, accomplishing her personal goal of stirring up memories. She hadn't missed the way Mr. Ivey wrapped an arm around his wife and squeezed her tenderly at that shared memory.

Hannah sighed. One day she'd have someone look at her that way, hold her close like that. She'd make memories with a man that she loved, memories that they could share for a lifetime. In other words, she'd have exactly what her mother had wished for on the day she died.

Have mercy, she couldn't wait. *God, if it be Your will, don't make me wait too long.*

Hannah was still imagining that day, that man, when she had the strong sensation that she was being watched. That was the thing about working in windows. *She* was on display, too.

Turning, she found a beautiful little girl, her long brown curls pulled up in two pigtails and her dark eyes sparkling as she gazed toward the window. Pulling on the hand of her father, she edged closer. Hannah smiled at her reaction and was instantly proud that her display had caused such palpable enthusiasm in this child.

The little girl pointed at Hannah and said something to her father, who seemed genuinely mesmerized by his daughter. He was totally absorbed by her every word, as though there was nothing more important in the world than what she had to say.

Hannah's heart tugged at the scene. She crooked her finger and motioned for them to come inside and see the display, not only because she wanted the little girl to have a better view, but also because she wanted to get a firsthand look at the closeness these two shared.

A pang shot to Hannah's heart as they made their way around the side of the window and through the toy store's front door. When Hannah was about that little girl's age, she had spent afternoons at the square with her father. Daddy-daughter days, that's what he'd called it back then. She'd also had her mommy-and-me days with her mom, and then the entire family would have family fun days, which included Hannah's older sister Jana. Daddy-daughter, mommy-and-me and family fun days had consumed Hannah's existence as a child.

When she was thirteen all of that changed, and their family had never been the same.

She blinked a couple of times, sniffed back the emotion that occasionally pressed its way to the surface with old memories, and found another smile for them as they passed through the curtain separating the display window from the rest of the store.

"Hi," Hannah said, primarily to the little girl, since she was still on her knees and the girl was eye level. "What's your name?"

She was even prettier than Hannah had realized, her dark eyes framed with a bounty of even darker lashes and her skin as smooth as the porcelain dolls in the toy store's wooden curios.

She gave Hannah a shy smile then stepped forward. "I'm Autumn."

Hannah heard her father's deep inhalation and

glanced up to see the man staring at the two of them. His face was filled with something close to awe, and Hannah wondered why he was so affected by her interaction with his little girl. Evidently he realized that Hannah noticed his reaction and that her attention was now on him.

"I'm Matt Graham," he said, and a light chuckle found its way into his words. "You'll have to forgive me, but I'm just—" he visibly swallowed "—very happy right now." He cleared his throat, shook his head then ran a hand through black wavy hair. "I'm sure that doesn't make a lot of sense, but Autumn hasn't smiled—" another clearing of his throat "—hasn't been this happy in quite a while, and I can't tell you what this means."

Matt Graham. She'd heard the name recently, but couldn't place it. However, it wasn't his name that held her interest. It was his statement. His little girl—Autumn—hadn't been happy in quite a while. She seemed happy now, beaming at Hannah.

"Well, Autumn, do you like the dollhouses?" Hannah asked.

The little girl opened her mouth, then closed it and smiled again. And Hannah realized that she'd barely noticed the dollhouses since entering the display area. Instead, she seemed more interested in...Hannah.

Hannah glanced up at Autumn's father and found herself drawn to the easy smile he had for his daughter, to the sky-blue eyes bordered with thick black lashes, and to the fact that those eyes glistened with emotion for his little girl. He was a striking man, not only in appearance but in the unharnessed emotion that seemed to shine from his very soul.

She silently told herself to get a grip. He was this little girl's father, a lady's husband, and Hannah had no right to notice his eyes, or his smile, or the way that his love for his little girl made her own heart flutter. One day, she'd have a husband and a child, and her husband would look at their son or daughter that way, the way he looked at his daughter now.

"Autumn? Do you like the dollhouses?" he asked, in an obvious effort to get her to respond to Hannah's question.

"Yes," she whispered, but again, she didn't look at the houses. And her next words didn't have anything to do with them at all. "You're like Mommy." Her dark eyes grew wider, and she moved closer to Hannah. Then she reached out and gently, with a feather-soft touch, as though she didn't know whether Hannah was real, pressed small fingers against Hannah's cheek. "You're like her."

Hannah didn't move, didn't breathe. The child was so embraced in the moment that she didn't dare break the connection.

Then Autumn's mouth quivered, and she blinked. "I miss her. I miss her every day."

Hannah looked up to the man who stood grounded to the spot and whose eyes were definitely wet now. He looked as though he wanted to say something, but he couldn't. And Hannah didn't need him to. She'd been around that look of sadness enough to know. Autumn, this precious little girl with eyes that appeared as though they'd seen a lifetime worth of sorrow, had already lost her mother.

Hannah fought for composure and attempted to keep her own feelings at bay, since her mind immediately catapulted to that day twelve years ago when she told her own mother goodbye for the last time. This little girl was so young. Hannah had been thirteen and still struggled each day to understand why her mother was gone. Autumn appeared to be five or six, about the same age as the children Hannah taught in her class at church.

God, please help her. And help me to help her. I know how much it hurts to lose a mom.

Autumn's palm was still on Hannah's cheek when Mr. Feazell drew back the curtain and announced, "Hannah, guess what? I found some!"

The little girl dropped her hand, and Hannah took a deep breath, the intense moment broken.

"Oh, hi," Mr. Feazell said to the pair. "I didn't hear the bell, didn't realize we had people checking out the display. How do you like it?"

Matt Graham nodded to the toy store owner, but only took his eyes away from Hannah and Autumn for the slightest second before looking back at them and answering, "It's amazing."

Hannah had no doubt that he wasn't talking about the dollhouse display.

"I know," Mr. Feazell said, completely unaware of the dual conversation taking place. "Hannah ran the idea by me, and I thought it'd be good, but I had no idea…" He shook his head. "It's uncanny how much it looks like the real square, isn't it? Hannah has a knack at really touching the heart of things, don't you think?"

"Definitely," Matt Graham answered.

Again, Hannah knew for certain that he wasn't talking about the dollhouses. And she *had* touched the heart of something here, but she didn't quite know what. All she knew was that this little girl had been sad, but now she seemed happy.

And as a result, so did the compelling man standing before her.

"Well, Hannah, I finally found these. They'll make it even more authentic for sure." Mr. Feazell stretched out his hand to display a palm filled with tiny geese.

Hoping to ease the tension in the room, Hannah gave Autumn a soft smile, then reached for the gaggle of geese in Mr. Feazell's hand. "They look perfect."

"I thought they'd be a nice touch since, you know, those geese are always hanging around. Hey, maybe you can even put some folks on benches around a fountain and maybe have some bread on the ground in front of the birds. Now that would be realistic, wouldn't it?"

"Yes, it would," Hannah agreed.

Mr. Feazell tilted his head and curled his lower lip in as he studied the little girl's father. "You look familiar," he said, tapping his chin, "but you're not from Claremont, are you?" Then, before he could answer, Mr. Feazell snapped his fingers. "Wait a minute. I remember. You're the new doctor in town, aren't ya? Over at the General Physicians Building, right?"

"Yes, I am. Nice to meet you," he said, extending a hand. "I'm Matt Graham."

Hannah now knew why his name had sounded familiar. She'd read the article in the paper about the new doctor in town and had been happy to learn that Claremont had a physician with "big city experience," as the paper had defined it, since he'd previously practiced medicine in Atlanta. She'd also been surprised at how young he'd looked, and how undeniably handsome. She'd seen her share of doctors over the years and none of them had looked anything like Matt Graham.

"Ted Feazell," Mr. Feazell said, shaking his hand. "I own the Tiny Tots Treasure Box."

"You have a nice store here."

"Thanks," Mr. Feazell answered. "Hey, I hear you're doing a good job over there at the center. I saw the write-up in the paper. Come from Atlanta, right?"

Obviously, Hannah wasn't the only one impressed that an experienced doctor had moved to town.

"Yes." He didn't offer anything more than that, and Mr. Feazell didn't press the issue.

"Well, we're glad you found your way to our little neck of the woods. Claremont is small, that's for sure, but it's got everything you need."

Matt Graham nodded and glanced at Autumn, now tenderly touching one of the geese in Hannah's hand. "I'm glad we found our way here, too." He smiled. "Very glad."

Hannah's skin tingled with his smile, and she wondered what had really brought Matt Graham—Dr. Graham—and his little girl to Claremont. Surely a doctor from Atlanta would know that there wouldn't be nearly as many patients in a town as small as Claremont.

But more than wondering why the new doctor had

come to town, Hannah also wondered how long it had been since he lost his wife and since Autumn had been without her mother. She had said that Hannah was "like Mommy." What did that mean? Did Hannah favor her mother? And if she did, would it really be smart for Hannah to try to help her? What if she got confused and actually thought that Hannah *was* her mother? And if Hannah did favor Autumn's mother, then didn't that mean that she also favored Matt Graham's wife?

She glanced at him, still looking directly at her with those sky-blue eyes, dark black lashes, mesmerizing smile. She'd been with her sister that day, when the article had come out in the paper. Jana had pointed to the photo and playfully asked if Hannah felt a cold or cough coming on. Or any other reason for her to go visit the town's attractive new physician.

Hannah realized she was staring, and what's more, so was he. She jerked her attention to the geese in her hand and asked, a little too loudly, "Autumn, would you like to put them by the fountain?"

Mr. Feazell chuckled. "Hannah, maybe you've been working too long. I haven't brought you the fountain yet. Remember, I wanted to try to find that three-tiered one, so it'd be like the one in the square?"

Hannah looked at the empty spot in the middle of the display where the fountain should go and felt the blood rush to her cheeks.

The old man laughed again and glanced over his shoulder. "You know, I did see another box of the miniature accessories in the middle of the store. Maybe that's where that fountain is. Tell you what, Autumn. That's your name isn't it—Autumn?"

She nodded, her long curls bobbing with the action.

"Would you like to come look at all of the things we have for dollhouses and maybe help me find that fountain for the display? I bet Hannah might even let you put the geese around it, assuming we find it okay." He grinned. "Sound good?"

Hannah knew Mr. Feazell was merely conducting business in his own way, showing off the toys that he thought would most appeal to the little girl. But Autumn smiled, and her father did too.

"Would you like to go look at the dollhouse things and try to help Mr. Feazell find that fountain?" he asked.

Autumn nodded, pressed her fingertips against Hannah's cheek again then turned to the toy store owner. Mr. Feazell grinned and held open the curtain for her to pass through, and Matt Graham gently patted her back as they left.

"I love you, honey," he said.

Autumn paused. She looked at him, then at Hannah, and then at her daddy again. "I love you, too."

One hand moved to Matt Graham's chin and stayed there as he watched Autumn walk away with Mr. Feazell.

The display area, which had seemed expansive all morning as she situated the mass of dollhouses, suddenly grew smaller as Hannah realized that she and Dr. Matt Graham were now alone.

She cleared her throat and stood, her knees popping loudly from kneeling so long. He didn't seem to notice and appeared more intent to use this opportunity to talk to her than to comment on her noisy joints.

"Your name is Hannah?" he asked.

She was a little embarrassed at the fact that she hadn't thought to introduce herself. "Yes, Hannah Taylor."

He shifted the curtain aside and glanced into the store. Then he let the thin navy fabric fall back into place. "I didn't want her to hear," he said softly. "But I want to explain." He breathed in, let it out. "Autumn hasn't smiled and has barely spoken since we lost her mother. So when she smiled at you, when she spoke to you…" He pulled the curtain aside and glanced at his daughter again, then turned back to Hannah. "It was like watching a miracle. It's been two years."

Two years.

"Do I look like her mother?" In Hannah's mind, that was the only reasonable answer for why the child would have come out of her shell today.

But he shook his head. "No. Rebecca had long curly red hair." He smiled, obviously remembering his wife. "And lots of freckles." Then his eyes seemed to be drawn to Hannah's shirt, or more precisely, to the small pin on her left chest. "Rebecca had breast cancer."

Hannah swallowed past the lump in her throat, and her hand instinctively moved to the pink ribbon pin. "You think she saw my pin from out there?"

"I don't know, but somehow you reminded her of Rebecca." He indicated the pin. "You're a survivor, aren't you? You've had breast cancer, too." His eyes moved to her short hair, still growing back from her last round of chemo and radiation.

"I am. Actually, my sister and I are both survivors," Hannah said, always finding it easy to smile with the thrill that they were both in remission now. "But we also lost our mother to breast cancer, like Autumn. So I know how much it hurts."

He tilted his head, curiosity at Autumn's awareness still evident on his face. "Well, for some reason, she was drawn to you. Whether it was the pin or not, I can't say. But you got more words from her in the last ten minutes than three child psychologists did in two years." He paused. "Or than I have, since her mama died."

Hannah remembered her silent prayer, asking God to let her help this little girl. He'd undoubtedly granted her request. "Maybe because I'm meant to help her? God has His plans, you know."

That made him smile, and Hannah couldn't deny the impact that his smile had on her heart.

"Just now, when she told me that she loved me…" He inhaled, let it out, and seemed too overwhelmed to finish.

"She hasn't told you that she loves you," Hannah said, "in two years?"

He shook his head, looked as though he wanted to say more, but remained silent.

"Bless your heart," Hannah whispered.

He stepped closer. "I know this will sound a little odd, but I think maybe you're right. Maybe the reason I picked this town, the reason Autumn and I are here, is because of you."

Hannah's mind reeled with the statement. What was she supposed to do now? What was she supposed to say?

Thankfully, his laughter broke through her dilemma.

"I'm sorry. I can't imagine how that made you feel. It's just that I've been hoping, praying for a breakthrough for so long, and then all of a sudden, out of nowhere, here you are, and Autumn speaks. And smiles. It's… Well, I'd have to say it's an answered prayer. And in all honesty, I haven't prayed a lot in the past two years. Didn't really have a reason to trust in the power of it anymore."

Hannah found herself relaxing again. This was something she could relate to, because of her own father. "But now?" she asked, still wondering what role God planned for her to have in his daughter's life. And, maybe, in this man's life?

"Now I'm thinking I may need to send up a prayer of thanks," he said, grinning.

A rush of elation filled Hannah, and she was shocked with the undeniable excitement of the request God had granted. Autumn had been silent for two years. She'd been sad and quiet, and Hannah had no doubt that her unhappiness had caused Matt Graham to be unhappy, too. But today she'd smiled.

And so did he.

Hannah made a conscious decision to try to make both of them smile again. If God had given her this gift, then she intended to use it to her fullest ability.

Mr. Feazell yanked open the navy curtain barrier and entered the display area with Autumn by his side. She walked directly to Hannah and handed her a small three-tiered fountain.

"Here," she said, grinning with obvious enthusiasm that they'd found the perfect fountain. And it did look exactly like the one that centered two large oak trees in the town square.

"Thank you," Hannah said, then she motioned to the square gray area in the center of the display. "Can you place it in the middle there? Then you can put the geese around it, like they are in the square."

"Okay." Autumn concentrated on putting the fountain in the right spot, while Mr. Feazell moved between Hannah and Matt.

"Well, that's good," he said softly, watching Autumn situate the geese around the tiny fountain.

"The fountain?" Hannah asked.

"No, her talking," he said. "She never said a word while we were back there searching through all of that stuff, and I wasn't sure she could hear me there for a second. Glad she's okay." The bell sounded on the front door. "Hey, more customers," he said excitedly then darted back through the curtain.

Hannah watched Matt Graham's eyes soften toward his daughter before he looked back at Hannah. "She's only talking around you," he mouthed, and Hannah feared he was right.

Now she understood that God had done more than merely grant her request. He'd given her a challenge, and she nodded, determined not to let Him—or Matt Graham—down.

"Autumn, I have a lot to do if I'm going to finish this display before the First Friday celebration next week," Hannah said. "Do you think you could come here each afternoon after school and help me out, if it's okay with your daddy? I could sure use your help."

Matt nodded his approval at this suggestion.

"And you can come anytime you want tomorrow," Hannah added, "since it's Saturday. I'll be here most of the day."

Autumn's smile claimed her face. "Can I, Daddy? Please?"

"I believe that could be arranged," he said. "If Ms. Taylor is sure that we won't be in her way."

"Hannah. You can call me Hannah, Dr. Graham."

"I'd like that," he said, "but only if you call me Matt."

"Okay," she said, unable to hold back a grin. "Matt. And no, you won't be in my way at all."

"Then I'd love to bring Autumn to help."

Autumn stood and wrapped her arms around his legs. "Thank you," she whispered.

He scooped her up and held her close, kissed the side of her head and looked directly at Hannah. He didn't say a word, but his eyes said it all. Dr. Graham—Matt—was getting his little girl back, because of Hannah. And because God had granted her request, an opportunity to help Autumn. "Thank you, Hannah," he said. "You have no idea how much this means to her, and to me."

Hannah's heart hummed with excitement as the two left the display area. She looked at the new world she'd created with the array of dollhouses and thought about Autumn's world, and how it'd become a little bit brighter today after her visit to the toy store. After her visit with Hannah. Hannah had made her smile. And she'd made Matt Graham, the handsome doctor, loving daddy and undeniably intriguing man smile, too.

Thank you, God.

Chapter Two

"It just doesn't seem right, that they'd make you wait through the weekend. I never understood that. Those doctors did it that way with your mother, and I told them back then how frustrating it was, but they still did it, and now they're doing it again with Jana and with you. I guess they do it to everybody. But it isn't right to leave people hanging like that." Bo Taylor sat on the cushioned visitor bench in the display area while Hannah gathered the craft paints she'd need for the next dollhouse, the town square's candy shop.

"Daddy, sometimes it takes several days for the labs to complete the test results. And if my appointment is near the weekend, they can't help it that the testing isn't done before the end of their workweek. I'm sure the doctor will call Monday or Tuesday." She eyed the candy store dollhouse then glanced out the toy store's window to see the real Sweet Stop Candy Shop across the square. Her replica still needed an awning, patio tables outside and candy displays inside, but she should get all of that taken care of today with Autumn and Matt Graham's help. Hannah couldn't wait for them to arrive. She'd been looking forward to seeing the little girl all morning. And truthfully, she also looked forward to seeing Matt Graham. In fact, she hadn't stopped thinking about the handsome doctor since he left yesterday.

"Hannah? Did you hear me?" Her father gave her a frown and lifted one dark brow, a look that said he'd been waiting for her response, and of course, she'd been so absorbed in thinking about Matt and Autumn Graham that she hadn't heard the question.

"What did you say, Daddy?"

"I said I simply can't stop worrying about you and your sister, and these doctors don't make it any better by making us wait when you get those tests done every three months."

"Well, after this set of screenings, I'll have been a year in remission," Hannah happily reminded, "then I'll only get tested every six months, so you won't have to worry so often. And Jana only gets hers done annually now. If I keep getting clear results, I'll eventually move to that category, too." She grinned. "Hey, maybe then we can set up our tests on the same day, and you'll only have to worry once a year." She laughed.

He didn't. "You just wait until you have kids one day. You'll see how easy it is not to worry," he said, pointing a finger at her and squinting one eye to punctuate the statement. "You'll see, when you have kids."

Hannah instantly remembered Autumn's hand against her cheek and recalled the warmth that spread through her at that sweet child's touch. "I'm looking forward to it."

He smiled. "Yeah, well, kids make it worth the

worry. And we'll have another little one soon, won't we? With Jana's baby, I mean. I was so worried when she told us she was having a baby, but I admit I can't wait for that little girl to get here. Thank goodness her pregnancy has gone well…so far."

Hannah put down the paints, turned toward him and rested a hand on his knee. Her mother, Dee, had been the worrier in the family. After she passed away, Bo Taylor had taken over the role. "Daddy, Jana's baby will be here any day. The doctor says that little Dee is healthy and that Jana is doing great, so there's nothing to worry about there either."

"I know," he said, looking a little guilty for always being so troubled, "but I'll breathe a little easier when that little angel is here, safe and sound."

Hannah hated it that her father had such a hard time finding peace of mind. It would be so much easier if he'd somehow find a little of the faith he'd lost when her mother died. Hannah thought of Matt Graham and his words from yesterday.

"In all honesty, I haven't prayed a lot in the past two years. Didn't really have a reason to trust in the power of it anymore."

She'd understood what he meant, because she'd watched it firsthand with her father. If he'd turn his worries over to God, he'd be a lot happier, a lot calmer. She'd tried time and time again over the past twelve years to get him back in church, to help him find a relationship with God again. *That* was what he needed more than anything, and Hannah wasn't ready to stop trying to help him yet.

"Daddy, why don't you come to church tomorrow?

We're having the annual fall fellowship on the grounds after the morning service." She squeezed his knee. "It'd be good for you."

He scrubbed a hand down his face. "I don't know, Hannah."

"Think about it," she said, "for me, and for Jana and the new baby. You know we'll all be attending church every week, me, Jana, Mitch and baby Dee. You know you'll want to sit beside all of us on the pew every Sunday."

He lifted one corner of his mouth in a half grin. "You aren't ever going to give up on getting me there, are you?"

"Don't plan on it."

The other side of his mouth joined in and he gave her a smile. "I'll think about it."

"Good." Hannah turned toward the candy store dollhouse, picked up the red-and-white-striped awning she'd found for the entrance and ran a bead of craft glue along the top. Then she placed it above the shop's entrance and held it to bond. She glanced at her father and saw that he'd leaned his head back against the wall, closed his eyes and set his mouth in a tight, firm line. She assumed he was trying to decide what to do about church. Hannah thought he'd come close to returning to God a few times over the past decade, but something always held him back. Maybe a new baby in the family and thoughts of the future would prompt him to return.

God, help him come back to church. Help him come back to You.

She reached for a paintbrush to put the store's name on the redbrick building and then heard her father's deep sigh. Placing the brush back in the glass cup, she sat back on her knees to look at him.

He was forty-nine now, his hair still dark for the most part, with a patch of silver at each temple and a bit sprinkled above his ears. His build was that of a man who jogged daily, because that was one of his rituals since Hannah's mother had passed, running several miles each morning to relieve the stress. He had a healthy tan and was dressed neatly in a pale blue button-down shirt, jeans and the same style of light tan work boots that he'd worn as long as she could remember.

By all appearances, her father was a nice-looking man with Richard Gere appeal who should be enjoying life to the fullest. Except for the fact that he'd become a widower at thirty-seven and had to raise two daughters that were merely thirteen and fifteen at the time, and who both eventually ended up with the very disease that had taken his wife.

When he opened his eyes, their dark depths showed the sadness of those final facts and the reasons that he didn't enjoy life anymore, the reasons that he didn't trust in faith, or love, or for that matter, God, anymore.

"I want you back at church tomorrow, Daddy," she said. "It'd mean a lot to me, and I think it'd do a world of good for you, too." She waited, and when he didn't speak, she whispered, "Say yes, Daddy. Please."

He looked at her, but remained silent.

"Okay then, say maybe."

He smiled. "Maybe."

The bell on the door sounded, and Mr. Feazell called out a greeting to the incoming customers. "Well, hello,

Dr. Graham. How are all of you doing today?" The store owner proceeded to announce that his new puppets had arrived that morning, and then Hannah heard him direct them to the back of the store, where he'd set up a small stage for children to practice with the marionettes. Mr. Feazell had been eager to get every child's opinion on the new setup.

Her pulse skittered. She'd been looking forward to this all day and wanted her father to realize that Autumn and Matt Graham were special. "Daddy, there's a little girl I'm trying to help," she whispered, hoping her voice wouldn't carry far beyond the curtain barrier between the display and the store. "I just heard her arrive, and I'd like for you to meet her and her father. Her name is Autumn, and her father is Matt Graham, the new doctor in town." She paused, not wanting to make her father uncomfortable but wanting him to understand how important this was and how much she wanted to help Autumn. "Daddy, she lost her mother to breast cancer two years ago."

"How old is she?" he asked, keeping his deep voice low as well, undoubtedly realizing that Hannah didn't want this conversation overheard by the newcomers to the toy store.

"I believe she's five or six. She's in school, probably kindergarten or first grade. Anyway, her father brought her in yesterday, and she spoke to me, connected with me." Hannah watched him nod as though he totally understood, but she knew he couldn't until she told him the rest. "And then he told me that she hadn't spoken more than a word or two at a time since her mother died."

Bo Taylor frowned. "That's terrible."

"But she did yesterday, for me. She talked to me, smiled for me. I—" Hannah tried to form the right words to explain it "—I felt a connection between me and that little girl, Daddy. She needs someone who understands what she is going through. She needs me to help her cope with losing her mom." Hannah leaned forward so she could peek through the tiny crack in the display area's curtain and saw that Matt, Autumn and an older woman were all still listening to Mr. Feazell describe the elaborate puppet area. When she was certain they couldn't hear their conversation, she dropped the curtain back in place.

"Five or six," her father said. "And already lost her mom." He sighed wearily.

"She said that I'm like her mommy. I don't know if it's because she saw my breast cancer pin, or maybe because my hair is shorter, or what. But because she sees me as someone 'like her mommy,' she's willing to open up to me. Daddy, it touched my heart so much, I can't even explain it. I've been thinking about her all day." Hannah didn't add that she'd also been thinking about Matt Graham all day. Or the fact that he fell into the same category as her father, losing a wife to breast cancer and being left to raise a child, even if Matt only had one to raise and her father had been left with two.

However, looking at her father's face now, Hannah suspected that her dad also put the similarities together and could literally feel the little girl's pain...and, of course, Matt Graham's pain.

"Daddy, I really think I can help her. I think I'm meant to."

He pinched the bridge of his nose. "Bless her little heart," he whispered. "Bless her precious little heart."

"I don't know why she picked me to talk to, but I prayed to God to let me help her, and I think He is letting me do that." She noticed her father's face alter a fraction when she mentioned her prayer, but he didn't say anything negative. "She's going to start coming here every day to help me with the display."

"I'm glad you're able to help her, princess," he finally said. "I just wish… I wish that no child had to go through that, and I wish you and your sister would have had someone to help you cope with everything back then. The way you're helping this little girl."

Hannah edged toward her father and took his hands in hers. It didn't take but a moment to realize his were trembling. "Daddy, we did have someone to help. We had God, and we had you. And we made it through."

Mr. Feazell's voice grew louder as he directed the Grahams back to the front of the store. "Well, I think Hannah's been working on a section of the town square today that you should all enjoy, the Sweet Stop. It's the candy shop straight across the square, you know."

Hannah gave her father a smile, released his hands then turned in time to see Mr. Feazell slide the curtain open and the trio of customers come into view. The woman with them appeared to be in her late forties and was very pretty, petite with short, wavy auburn hair. She tenderly patted Autumn's shoulder as they neared.

Autumn stood between her father and the woman, but she stepped in front of them as soon as she saw Hannah. "We came back," she said, her smile stretching across her face and her dark brown eyes growing wide with excitement. She had her hair pulled up in a high ponytail with a navy bow. A waterfall of long brown curls trailed past her shoulders, and she wore a plaid navy-and-green jumper over a white shirt. Even her Mary Jane shoes were navy leather, cute over white kneesocks.

She was absolutely adorable, and Hannah fought the urge to reach out, pull her into her arms and simply hold her, to let her know that everything would be okay again. She didn't want to scare her away, but she truly wanted Autumn to know how much she cared. Eventually they would work their way to a hug greeting. Hannah hoped so, anyway.

"Hello, Hannah," Matt said. "I had a patient to see this morning, or we'd have been here earlier. Still okay for us to help you out today? I think Autumn's been looking forward to it ever since we left yesterday."

"Of course it's still okay, and I've been looking forward to it too," Hannah said, smiling at Autumn.

"This is my mother-in-law, Maura," Matt continued, indicating the woman beside him.

"Nice to meet you," Hannah said.

"Wonderful to meet you," Maura replied. "Really wonderful. Matt told me about yesterday, and well, I wanted to come too. I hope that's okay."

"It's fine," Hannah said. She touched her dad's hand. "This is my father, Bo Taylor."

Maura and Matt exchanged greetings with Hannah's father, while Autumn's attention zeroed in on the dollhouse that Hannah had pulled out from the remainder of the display.

"Is that the candy store?" she asked, pointing to the dollhouse in progress.

"It sure is."

Maura's hand moved to her mouth and she shook her head in apparent awe at Autumn's communication with Hannah.

"That's GiGi," Autumn said, pointing to Maura.

And at her granddaughter's words, Maura's eyes trickled silent tears. "She couldn't say grandma when she started talking," Maura explained, "and I became GiGi." She smiled warmly toward Autumn. "But I haven't heard her say it in a long time." Her voice broke with that declaration, but Autumn didn't notice, still smiling at Hannah.

Hannah wasn't sure what to say in response to Maura's statement, so she instead spoke to Autumn. "I put that awning on a couple of minutes ago." She pointed to the newest addition to the structure. "Do you like it?"

Autumn followed Hannah's finger and grinned. "Yes." Then she looked over Hannah's shoulder to gaze out the window and across the square. "It looks like that one."

Hannah followed her line of sight and saw that she'd spotted the Sweet Stop and the red-and-white-striped awning covering the entrance. "That's right. And I want this little shop to look just like that big one."

"I can help you do that," Autumn said.

Maura moved her hand to Matt's arm and gently squeezed. Then Hannah heard her whisper, "It's a miracle."

Hannah reached for the bag of candy she'd tucked

beside the dollhouses. "You know, I also need someone to help me eat the treats Mr. Feazell brought in from the Sweet Stop today."

The doorbell sounded, and Mr. Feazell laughed. "Well, you guys eat the sweets, and I'll go check on the other customers." He released the curtain and returned to the store.

"You have candy?" Autumn asked, peering over Hannah's shoulder as she reached for the bag.

"I sure do." Hannah held the sack open so Autumn could see inside. "And I have enough for everyone."

Hannah's father patted his hand to his stomach and smiled. "No sweets for me today," he said, "and I'm going to head on out." He looked back at Matt and Maura. "Pleasure to meet both of you."

"And you," Matt said.

Then Bo looked at Hannah and Autumn, and Hannah noticed how his attention focused on the little girl, fingering through the sweets in the bag.

"I'm going over to Mitch and Jana's house later," he said to Hannah. "She said she's cooking lasagna and wants us all to come. I think she got some new pictures of the baby yesterday at her ultrasound appointment. You coming?"

"She asked me as well," Hannah said. "And she told me about the ultrasound pictures. I wouldn't miss it."

He nodded, glanced again at Autumn. "Nice to meet all of you," he repeated, then left.

Autumn looked up from the bag, where she'd found a fluffy piece of divinity wrapped in pink cellophane and tied with an orange ribbon. "Do you get candy every day?" she asked, tugging on the bow and opening the candy. She took a small bite and grinned. "Because I think I'd like to come back, every day."

Hannah laughed. "I don't get candy every day, but I get a bag of treats fairly often. Life's a little better when there's sugar in it, or that's what my mama always said." She heard Matt's chuckle.

"I think I'd have to agree with that," Maura said.

"Well, I'd like to come every day anyway," Autumn said, her words a little muffled with more of the sweet white candy in her mouth.

Hannah grinned. "Good, because that's what I'd like, too."

"I believe that's a great idea," Maura said. "Absolutely wonderful idea."

"You want one?" Autumn asked, holding the bag toward Hannah.

"I never turn down candy from the Sweet Stop." Hannah pulled out a piece of divinity, this one wrapped in blue cellophane and tied with a yellow ribbon.

"You want one, GiGi?" Autumn asked, and Maura nodded enthusiastically, her happiness at hearing her name from her granddaughter evident in her smile.

"Do you, Daddy?"

"Yes, precious," he said, and withdrew a green-and-white-striped candy apple stick.

While they enjoyed the candy, a few people stopped at the window and waved. Hannah and Autumn waved back, while Matt and Maura smiled from the small visitor's bench. Then Hannah passed out some hand cleaning wipes to get the stickiness off before she and Autumn continued working on the newest dollhouse addition to the town square display.

"Okay, here's our plan," she said to Autumn, while she ran the cool wipe over her fingers. "I'm going to work on the outside of the store, paint the name on the building, place the patio arrangements, put flower boxes beneath the windows and all of that. Your job is to go through these things that Mr. Feazell brought us and pick what you want to put inside the store. It doesn't have to be exactly like the candies in the store, but we want it to be as close as possible, okay?"

Autumn nodded, intently listening to every word. "Okay."

Hannah held up a tiny glass case. "This display case looks like the one in the store. You'll want to put some of the tiny candies inside, and we've got plenty to choose from. Mr. Feazell even found small pictures that look like the paintings that hang in the Sweet Stop. I'll let you pick which ones to hang on the walls."

Again Autumn nodded and began looking through the tiny items.

"There may be one problem with your plan," Matt said.

Hannah looked up and found herself face-to-face with the man who, at some point in the past few seconds, had moved from the bench to the floor. Sitting merely a couple of feet away, he looked completely comfortable on the floor, not doctorlike at all, like a dad wanting to be involved in the activity his daughter enjoyed. And like a guy that a girl would enjoy having around, to sit beside her and simply be a part of her life. He was close enough that Hannah could smell the crisp scent of his aftershave, or his soap, or whatever it was that tickled her nose and seemed so undeniably masculine.

It'd been quite a while since she'd been this close to a man, or at least a man that she found this attractive, and she wasn't prepared for the excited nervousness that went along with the proximity. His eyes, Hannah now noticed, were focused on her, and she had to concentrate to remember what he'd said. Then she blinked, replayed the last couple of minutes, and had it.

"A problem?" she managed.

"Autumn hasn't been inside the Sweet Stop. We've been to the square a couple of times since we moved here, but we never went in the shop. I honestly didn't even think about it," he admitted, then smiled and added, "I try to watch sweets, being a doctor and all, but I do like them." He held up the candy stick. "And I should have realized that Autumn would, too." He shrugged. "Don't know why that didn't occur to me."

Hannah's heart clenched in her chest. Bless his heart, he had no idea that Autumn wanted to go to the Sweet Stop because until yesterday, she hadn't said enough words for him to know.

"Well, that is a problem," Hannah said, glancing at Autumn.

The little girl's head tilted to the side and her smile faded. "So I can't do it? I can't put the things inside the store?" She paused, her mouth tightening. "I can't help you?"

"No, baby, that's not it," her daddy said, and he reached in his back pocket, withdrew his wallet and fished out a few dollars. "You can definitely do it, but it'd be easier if you were able to see the store from the inside. So why don't we go over and let you take a look before you try to decorate the little one here? We can even take some pictures with my phone, so you can look at them when you're picking the things out for your store."

Pride illuminated Autumn's face when he said "your" store, and the sight of it thrilled Hannah. She was such a pretty little girl, and absolutely breathtaking when she smiled.

"And while we're there," Matt continued, "we'll get some sweets to take home. I haven't had nearly enough candy in the house, and every little girl needs candy every now and then. Because—" he grinned "—I have it from a very reliable source that life's a little better with sugar in it."

A frisson of pure happiness shimmied down Hannah's spine with his words and his smile.

"Okay!" Autumn said, standing. "Let's go get candy!"

"Can I take her?" Maura asked, her tone almost pleading. "I want to pick out some sweets for home, too."

Matt had been preparing to stand, but stopped and eased back down near Hannah. "Sure," he said, handing over the bills and his cell phone to Maura. "Just make sure you get me some, too," he said with a laugh.

"Thank you, William. I truly appreciate this," Maura said, reaching her palm toward her granddaughter. Hannah noticed that she referred to Matt as William, but he didn't seem to acknowledge the error, so she didn't let it register on her face, either. Maura gave

Autumn a timid smile. "You want to go get some candy with GiGi?"

"Yes," Autumn said, placing her hand in her grandmother's and then telling Hannah and Matt, "We'll be right back."

Maura beamed with delight.

"That sounds great," Matt answered. "And make sure you get some more of these apple candy sticks. I've got a feeling I'm going to want another one later."

"We will," Autumn said.

Hannah waited until they exited the toy store and she and Matt had waved to them before they headed across the square. Then she said, "I didn't think about the possibility that she hadn't been in the Sweet Stop yet. I should have thought of that, since you haven't lived here that long."

"No need for you to apologize. I should have thought about the possibility that she would have wanted to go in the candy store," he said, rolling the green apple candy stick between his thumb and forefinger as he spoke. "I took her all around the square yesterday hoping to find something she liked and didn't even think of the candy store."

"You're a doctor," Hannah said. "Sweets probably aren't as high up on your list as they are on everyone else's, or at least mine."

He smirked at that. "Hey, I'll have you know I like candy as much as the next guy. I just try to be smart about it." He popped the end of the green apple stick in his mouth.

"Well, I'll have *you* know that I try to eat a little candy every day," Hannah said, reaching back into the bag and withdrawing another piece of divinity. She peeled back the wrapper and popped the whole thing in her mouth without getting an inkling of stickiness on her fingers. But her mouth was now full, and he noticed.

"You know, I wasn't going to try and take it from you," he said, laughing.

She started to speak but couldn't and held up a finger while she chewed. Eventually, while he kept laughing, she swallowed then also laughed. "I didn't think you would," she clarified. "I was simply trying to get it all in my mouth with the cellophane so my hands wouldn't be sticky while I work."

"Sure you were."

Hannah's skin tingled at their easy, flirty banter. Here he was, a nice guy—a doctor, no less—with a sense of humor, an amazing smile and an adorable little girl that had already touched Hannah's heart. She could really get used to this.

"You said yesterday that you and your sister are both in remission," he said.

"Yes, we are," Hannah said with a grin. "Isn't that wonderful?"

"Definitely. And your dad mentioned she's having a baby?"

"She's due in a few weeks," Hannah said. "I think he was worried about her getting pregnant, because of the cancer and all, but everything has gone very well. I think Dad was afraid that if something happened and her cancer came back, then she wouldn't be able to get treated during the pregnancy, or it would hurt the baby, or something like that. But she hasn't had any problems at all."

"I'm glad she hasn't had any problems." He paused, seemed to think about something, and then said, "Even if something would have happened and she had needed treatments, it's believed that treatment after the first trimester is still safe for the baby."

"Really? I'm sure they probably talked to Jana about it, but she never told me that. I guess I assumed you'd have to wait until after you had the baby to keep the baby from getting hurt by the treatment." She shrugged. "I'm sure our family spends a lot of time thinking about things like that when we don't need to worry. Especially since Jana is doing great," she added with a smile.

"I think any time you've been affected by a disease, you think about it. I'm glad Jana's doing well. And I'm glad that you are doing well, too. Very glad."

"Me too."

He glanced out the window toward the Sweet Spot, where Hannah could see Autumn's dark curls through the store's window. She stood by the candy display case and pointed to something, and Maura held the phone up to take a picture. "Our family has been affected by that disease, too, I'm sure you can tell," he said. "But this past week has been an answer to our prayers in helping us deal with everything. It's amazing, seeing Autumn like this, happy again." He paused. "I told Maura about her breakthrough yesterday, and she wanted to come today. I assumed it'd be okay."

"Of course."

He eyed the bag of candy then peeked inside.

Hannah laughed. "Go on, I know you want to try something else."

"With the way you wolfed down that divinity, I thought I'd be lucky if there was another piece left."

"There are three pieces left, thank you very much," she said, handing him one of the remaining candies.

He smiled, unwrapped the divinity and followed her method of popping the whole thing in his mouth. Then he held up a hand to show her he'd also managed the feat without a bit of stickiness.

"Good job," she said, admiring not only his manner for eating the candy without getting sticky, but also the way he looked so appealing accomplishing the task.

He finished chewing and swallowed. "Thanks. I have a feeling I learned from the master."

She laughed again, put down the bag of candy and picked up a tiny flower box. "Okay, but I need to take a break from eating candy now and get back to the job."

He fingered the small patio pieces. "I know we're causing you to work extra hours on this display, and I want to apologize for that."

Hannah smiled. Here he was, finally finding his daughter again after two years and concerned that Hannah's part in it all was something of a burden. On the contrary. Hannah thought it nothing short of a blessing, or maybe even a miracle, like Maura had said, but definitely not a burden.

"No apology necessary. I'm not exactly on the clock when I work. I quote a price for a window display, and then I work whatever hours it takes to complete the project." She shrugged. "I usually try to take my time, because people like watching me work in the window."

"I can understand why people want to watch you," he said.

"Yeah, I think people find it enjoyable to get a bird's-eye view of something being created. It's kind of like watching through the window at the Sweet Spot and seeing how the doughnuts are made, the cookies are decorated and all of that. I think I could watch them all day."

"You do like sweets, don't you?"

She smiled. "Very much."

He smirked. "I see, but I wasn't talking about watching you work. The reason I can understand why people want to watch you is because I also find it enjoyable—" blue eyes lifted and found hers "—looking at you."

Hannah noted the intensity of his tone and the fact that he now looked at her in a way that made her feel very feminine, very pretty. She felt herself blush, and glanced away.

"Didn't mean to make you feel uncomfortable," he said. "Just stating the facts. Kind of goes along with my profession, you know."

"It shouldn't make me uncomfortable," she said, fiddling with the miniature flowers for the window boxes. "But I'm out of practice at hearing those kinds of compliments, I suppose."

"You aren't used to hearing compliments? Really? Why is that?"

She was thrown by the genuine surprise in his tone. However, instead of finding his question too personal and feeling awkward, for some reason, she found it easy to talk to him, even about things that she rarely admitted. Maybe it was because he'd been through similar circumstances, dealing with breast cancer and losing someone he cared about, but for whatever reason, Hannah didn't hide the truth. She, like him, stated the facts.

"Because of my cancer. I didn't want to get close to someone and then put them in the situation of going through those treatments, then all of that waiting and wondering and hoping. So I've kept to myself the past few years." She shrugged. "The past three years, in fact, ever since I was diagnosed. No dating or anything like that. It'd have been too difficult with everything going on in my life."

A look passed over his face, but Hannah couldn't read it, and she didn't know how to ask him what he was thinking. So she did what she often did when she found herself in an uncomfortable moment within a conversation; she changed the subject.

"So anyway, I get paid for the job, regardless of how much time it takes. And sometimes the owners even throw in bonuses if I'll take a little longer."

"Bonuses?"

She held up the bag of candies. "Like today, Mr. Feazell brought these in."

He grinned at that. "I see, a bonus."

She nodded. "Definitely."

He looked out the window and evidently noticed Maura and Autumn leaving the candy store. Then he edged a little closer, not close enough to invade her personal space, but close enough that Hannah could see that his eyes had a deep navy border around the edges and that the contrasting hue only made the clear blue center that much more vivid. He lowered his voice and said, "I should tell you this before they get back. Maura has lived with us ever since Rebecca died, and it's nearly destroyed her to lose her daughter and then, in a sense, lose Autumn, too."

Hannah nodded. "I saw how happy she was when Autumn said her name."

"That was an answered prayer for Maura." He inhaled deeply, exhaled. "This entire week has been like an answered prayer."

Occasionally Hannah sensed an opportunity, like God was putting her in a specific place and time to do something that was part of His plan. Right now she sensed that, and she wasn't going to let opportunity pass her by. "Tomorrow we're having our annual fall dinner on the grounds at church, the Claremont Community Church, after the morning worship service. The church is about a mile from the elementary school and fairly close to Hydrangea Park."

"I've seen the church," he said.

"You, Autumn and Maura should come."

The bell sounded on Mr. Feazell's door and within seconds Autumn bounded through the curtain's opening with a white paper sack bulging with candies. "We got lots more candy and GiGi took a bunch of pictures," she said.

Maura followed her into the tiny space, and it didn't take Hannah more than a moment to see that something had changed in the woman's disposition during the time she'd been away. Her eyes were moist with unshed tears, and her mouth quivered slightly.

Autumn didn't notice anything but Hannah, and Hannah kept her attention by surveying and marveling over all of the candy she had in the bag, while Matt stood and moved toward his mother-in-law. He held up a finger to Hannah, then he and Maura exited the display area and whispered outside.

The majority of their words were muttered so softly that Hannah couldn't make them out, and Autumn's exclamations about the candy drowned out a portion as well, but Hannah did catch enough to understand why her temperament had changed so dramatically during their walk to and from the Sweet Stop.

"She didn't say a thing, not to me or to the guy at the candy store. Not one word."

A few minutes later, Hannah heard the bell on the door again then saw Maura slowly walking toward the fountain in the center of the square. Autumn noticed, too.

"Where's GiGi going?"

Matt had returned to the display area and squatted down next to them on the floor. "GiGi is going to sit by the fountain and watch the geese for a little while," he said, but Hannah detected the sadness in his tone. She knew Maura had been upset that Autumn hadn't opened up to her, as well. But she would, eventually, if Hannah had her way.

God, let that be part of Your plan, that Autumn will open up to everyone, not just me. And help Maura be patient while she's waiting to reconnect with her granddaughter.

"She gave me the phone before she left," Matt said, extending the cell phone toward Hannah.

"Thanks." For a brief moment, Hannah's fingertips brushed against his as she took the phone. She glanced up, found that he also looked at the place where their skin touched. Hannah fumbled over the keys on the phone and tried to determine how to review the photos that Maura had taken.

"Here, let me help," he said, but instead of taking the phone from her, he eased his hand around hers and then guided her to the correct keys. "There they are. This arrow button will let you look through them, and you can zoom out with this one here."

Hannah swallowed, nodded. "Thanks."

"See that picture with all of the chocolate stuff," Autumn said, twisting to look at the phone's display. "That's the one I want to do first."

Hannah found the photo, zoomed it out and turned it so Autumn could see.

"Yes, that one." Autumn drew her brows together and rummaged through the box of tiny candies that Mr. Feazell had found this morning. Her tongue poked out the side of her mouth as she withdrew tiny chocolate cupcakes, a tray of fudge and some miniature chocolate-covered strawberries.

Hannah opened the back of the tiny display case for the candies, and Autumn began carefully placing the items inside. Hannah watched her situate a row of cupcakes. "You're doing a great job," she said.

"Thanks! What do you think, Daddy?" She turned the case to let him see the cupcakes, all lined up across the mini shelf.

"It's beautiful, sweetie," he said.

Autumn continued placing the cupcakes and candies, while Matt and Hannah worked together to praise her efforts and make sure she had whatever she needed to put the items in place. Matt also helped Hannah find additional faux flowers to match the ones in the windowsills above the candy store, and the two of them worked together to create the window boxes of cascading plants for the candy store dollhouse.

After about an hour, Matt stretched. "I've gotta stand up." He rose from the floor, and his knees cracked loudly.

Hannah laughed. "Guess you're used to standing when you work, huh?"

"Definitely," he said, rolling his neck as he spoke. He scanned the area outside the window and then asked, "Is that your father?"

Hannah followed his gaze to see Maura sitting on one of the benches near the fountain and next to her, Hannah's father. The two tossed bread toward a group of geese. Their heads moved as they talked, and she even saw her father laugh at something Maura had said. "Yes, that's Daddy. He used to go to the fountain regularly and feed the geese, but he doesn't come to the square that often anymore."

"He came today," Matt reminded.

She nodded. "He came today because he wanted to talk to me about my— Well, about some things that were bothering him. I guess he decided to feed the geese while he was here."

"Well, I'm glad they're visiting. Maura hasn't had an opportunity to meet too many people since we moved here. She mainly stays at the house and basically only leaves to take Autumn to and from school, go grocery shopping, that type of thing. She could use a friend, especially one that makes her smile."

Hannah saw that now both of them had their heads tossed back, and from the way her father pointed to one of the bigger birds, they were apparently laughing at something one of the geese had done. She smiled at the two of them. It was amazing, seeing her father actually laughing, appearing to enjoy himself, after so many years.

"You know," Hannah said, again deciding to jump on an opportunity, "Maura would meet a lot more people if y'all came to church. Especially tomorrow, since we're having the fall fellowship and all."

"Daddy? Can we? Can we go to church with Miss Hannah tomorrow?"

Hannah ran her palm down Autumn's silky curls. "Yeah, can you?" she teased.

He laughed. "How can I say no?"

"You can't!" Autumn said, standing and reaching toward her father to give him a hug.

He hugged her back. "You're right, precious. I can't." He peered over her shoulder to look at Hannah. "Okay, what time is the service, and what can I bring for that meal?"

"Ten o'clock, and I'm bringing plenty of food, so don't bring a thing."

"All right then, it's a date," he said.

"It's a date," Hannah repeated. And although it wasn't a date in the traditional sense of the word, with the way her heart was beating, she was even more excited.

Chapter Three

Matt woke Sunday morning realizing that Hannah Taylor had done something that he hadn't been certain was even possible anymore. She'd made him feel alive again, like he could have a chance at experiencing life again, experiencing a relationship again. Since he met her, he found himself thinking about her more often than not, hearing her laughter in his thoughts, seeing her smile, picturing the way her eyes darken when she's happy. And for the first time in two years, he imagined himself finding love again. No, not love with just any woman, but love with Hannah. He could see her beside him, growing closer to each other, and the two of them forging the type of relationship that would last a lifetime.

But there was a definite problem with any type of future Matt could visualize with Hannah Taylor, and that involved the words that had troubled him since yesterday afternoon, playing through his mind continually in a loop and keeping him awake for the majority of last night. Hannah's words.

"Because of my cancer, I didn't want to get close to

someone and then put them in the situation of going through those treatments, all of that waiting and wondering and hoping with me. So I've kept to myself the past few years."

By the time Matt, Maura and Autumn were in the car and headed to church, Hannah's statement had become a haunting declaration of the very reason that Matt could never have a relationship with the captivating woman.

"I can't go through that again," he said, more to himself than to anyone in the car.

Maura, ever observant, turned toward him and asked, "Can't go through what, William?"

"Matt," he corrected, and gave her a smile.

"Still can't get used to that, but I'm trying," she admitted. "But don't change the subject. Something's been bothering you all morning, and I didn't want to ask in front of Autumn, but since she's into her movie, I'd really like to know."

He glanced in the rearview mirror to see Autumn, settled in the backseat with her headset on and already picking up where she left off yesterday in *Finding Nemo.* Matt often wondered if the similarities between Autumn and the little fish were what drew her to her favorite movie. Nemo lost his mother and had a father who had a hard time connecting with his child and who definitely had a difficult time learning to trust again, to live again. Come to think of it, the similarities between Marlin, Nemo's dad, and Matt were pretty uncanny too.

"William?" Maura prodded then amended, "Matt? *What* can't you go through again?"

He lowered his voice, in case Autumn could hear beyond the headset. "Letting myself care," he said simply. But if he were completely honest, he'd have said, *"Letting myself love."*

Her mouth tightened, and she placed a hand on his shoulder. "You're talking about Hannah Taylor, aren't you? I thought I detected something between you two. It's been a long time since I saw that look in your eye, but I was fairly certain…"

"What look?" he asked, glancing at her momentarily but then quickly taking his eyes back to the road.

"The look you had toward Rebecca when you first met, the look that said you were fascinated by her and that you were thinking of her as something more than a friend." She squeezed his shoulder. "That *look*." When he didn't speak, she sighed. "Listen, there is no reason that you should spend the rest of your life alone. It isn't what Rebecca would have wanted, and it isn't what I want either, just in case you're wondering. You're a young, healthy man who should enjoy life to its fullest, and that beautiful sweet Hannah has obviously captured your interest, something no one else has done in two years, I'd guess. There's no reason you shouldn't ask her out."

"Yes, Maura, there is," he said, turning onto the road leading to the church.

She huffed out a breath. "Well, I'm listening. What is it?"

Matt decided there was no way to sugarcoat the facts, so he didn't try. "She has cancer. Breast cancer."

"She's in remission," Maura clarified.

He nodded. "Yes, but you and I both know that the

fact of the matter is that her cancer can come back. Do you really think that's anything I should put Autumn through again? Let her get attached to someone and then let her watch them die *again?*" He continued toward the church parking lot. No, he didn't want to put Autumn through it again, but he also couldn't put himself through it again.

Maura only hesitated for a moment before spouting her case. "So you're going to live your life in fear of losing someone you love again," she said, her tone resolute. "Everyone dies, William. Eventually we lose the ones we love. That's simply a fact of life. I lost Nolen ten years ago and Rebecca two years ago. I loved them both dearly, but I had to keep living. I had no choice. Life still goes on."

"Maura, that isn't what I'm talking about. This, with Hannah, is different. She has the potential to die of the exact same disease as Rebecca. I simply can't put Autumn through that again, let her get attached and love someone that way and then lose her again." He parked the car, motioned to Autumn to find a stopping place in the movie and waited for her to press the pause button before turning off the ignition.

"But don't you see?" Maura whispered. "Autumn is already attached to her. That's the whole reason we're going to see Hannah each day, because she's the only person Autumn has really connected with since we lost Rebecca. Either way, Autumn would be upset if anything happened to Hannah. But Hannah is in remission, and I certainly don't see why you should risk having a relationship again simply because of what *might* happen in the future."

He shook his head, about to argue his point a little more, but then he heard the unsnap of Autumn's seat belt. "Yay, we're here!" She leaned forward to stick her head between their seats and peer toward the church building. "And there's Miss Hannah!" And suddenly, just like that, Matt found himself looking toward the Claremont Community Church with the apprehension of a kid heading to the tree on Christmas morning, except it wasn't presents that he wanted to find.

It was Hannah.

"Yes, there she is," he responded, and he couldn't hold back a smile of appreciation at the exquisite woman standing near the church steps and waving at them.

Maura nodded. "In case you're wondering, *that's* the look I was talking about." She raised her brows and pointed to Matt's face.

Matt tried to think of a response, but luckily Autumn's excited squeal saved him.

"Look! She's wearing those shoes I like!"

He noticed the sparkly silver ballet slippers that Hannah had on the first day they'd seen her at the toy store. The remainder of her outfit was equally eye-catching. She wore a Kelly green short-sleeved sweater and a matching floral skirt. Something on the top left side of her sweater caught the sunlight and glistened, and he noted the pink ribbon pin, he assumed a staple in Hannah's daily wardrobe. She looked more spring than fall, even though today was the 2nd of October. But somehow, on Hannah, the look seemed to fit as a statement of life, the fact that she survived a battle and was still going strong, pushing forward and ready to live, like those bright spring flowers covering her skirt.

He recalled that same look of triumph on his patients' faces at the research center in Atlanta. Most of their faces, anyway. Occasionally, he saw another look, one of defeat. That was the look that hurt the most, especially the day he saw it on Rebecca's face. He didn't ever want to see that look on Hannah's face, which was why he didn't need to let his feelings toward her go beyond friendship. And it also meant that somehow he needed to control Autumn's closeness with Hannah.

Autumn quickly got out of the car. "Can I go ahead and see her? Please?"

How in the world would he ever curb Autumn's enthusiasm toward Hannah? And how could he, when Hannah was the only person who'd gotten his little girl out of her shell?

"Can I, Daddy?"

"Sure," he said, gathering their Bibles from the console. He looked at the shiny leather exteriors, hardly touched in the past two years. Thankfully, he'd known where they were on the bookshelf in his home office. He may not have been to church in a while, but he knew to bring the Good Book when he went.

The Good Book. That'd been Rebecca's term, and he'd adored the reverent phrase. She'd carried her Bible everywhere, right up until those last few months, when her faith began to waver. At the very end, however, during those last days, she'd found God again. But somewhere around that same time, Matt had lost Him. Looking at the steepled white building, the people gathering to worship together and the children happily chatting, he realized that he'd missed more than having someone special in his life. He'd missed all of this, missed having faith, missed having God.

"Maybe it's time," he said as he climbed from the car.

Like earlier, Maura didn't miss his statement. "Maybe it is," she agreed. She waited for him to make it around the front of the car and then joined him to walk toward the building. "I meant what I said before. Rebecca wouldn't have wanted you to be alone forever," she said, her words quietly spoken. "Maybe it *is* time." She looked toward Autumn, now hugging Hannah's legs. "Hannah Taylor is a beautiful young woman, and she has a good heart. You can see that just looking at her. Autumn obviously has been touched by her." She paused her steps. "And you can't make decisions about your future, and about Autumn's future, based on what-ifs. You're interested in Hannah, and you'd be a fool not to see where that interest will take you. It's been two years, and I agree that it *is* time for you to live again."

Matt was floored. "Maura, you misunderstood. I wasn't talking about dating again." He indicated the Bibles and held one out to her. "I was talking about this—church and God. I was saying that maybe it's time to come back to church, and back to Him."

Autumn's giggle lifted on the breeze and carried a burst of hope straight to his heart. His little girl was coming back to them, and he was thrilled.

Maura noticed him smiling at his daughter and at Hannah, who'd evidently said something about her shiny shoes that made Autumn laugh.

"Well, maybe it's time for all of it," she said, undeterred as she accepted the Bible. She ran a hand across the soft red leather. "Church, God…and living again. Dating again." She nodded pointedly, as though the matter had been decided.

Matt was grateful that the church members didn't mind passing them by in the parking lot and also didn't appear to hear any of this conversation as they moved toward the building. All said hello or nodded, or issued some other type of greeting as they passed, but they didn't eavesdrop, which was good, considering how uncomfortable he was with this conversation.

Maura tucked her Bible close to her chest. "I can tell you aren't in the mood to talk about it now."

"No, Maura, I'm not," he said then thought about how negative that sounded and how truly blessed he was to have her here. "But I do appreciate how concerned you are for me and for Autumn. You know that. Now, let's go catch up with Autumn and see if we can remember how all of this goes. It's kind of odd feeling like a fish out of water at church."

"I think you're making a mistake," she mumbled, but then her attention moved from Matt to Autumn and Hannah, waving at three people nearing them on the sidewalk. Bo Taylor walked beside a red-haired man and a pretty, very pregnant brunette. They all waved back and all three smiled, though Bo looked a bit apprehensive as he moved closer to the building.

Matt walked beside Maura and watched the family greet each other. The scene touched his heart, and he studied every detail. Hannah, reaching out to her father and hugging him, Bo Taylor's eyes pinching closed when he was in her embrace, the red-headed guy, obviously her sister's husband, draping his arm protectively around his wife. And Autumn, smiling and taking it all in.

Hannah's sister moved a hand to her rounded stomach, looked up at her husband and smiled. "This is a perfect day," she said to him, as Matt and Maura joined the group. Then to her father, "Thank you so much for coming, Daddy. Hannah said she thought you would be here today but, well, I guess I had to see for myself."

"Hannah was very persuasive," Bo Taylor said.

"I merely reminded him that he's going to miss out on the entire family—" she reached out and touched her sister's swollen belly "—being together at church every Sunday."

Bo Taylor nodded then looked toward Matt and Maura. "And I had a bit of encouragement from a new friend," he said.

Matt noticed Maura's blushing smile toward the man and wondered what all had transpired in their conversation by the town square fountain.

"You talked to my dad about going to church?" Hannah asked Maura.

Maura lifted a shoulder. "He said that was what was on his mind, your request that he go back to church, and I told him that I hadn't been in a while, either, and I missed it."

"You never told me that," Matt said.

"You didn't ask," she replied, then laughed. "It isn't your fault. I could have said something, and I guess I should have. But in any case, Bo and I talked about it, and I suppose we both decided *it was time*." Her emphasis on the last three words was unmistakable to Matt, but apparently the remainder of the group didn't notice.

"Well, I'm glad," Hannah's sister answered.

Hannah had a large pink-and-green tote bag filled with what appeared to be tiny fishing poles and a bunch of other odd shaped items, and she pulled the strap up higher on her shoulder. "Well, it's about time for me to start my class, but I want to introduce all of you before we head in. This is Mitch Gillespie, my brother-in-law, and my sister Jana." She turned to Matt. "And this is Dr. Matt Graham and his mother-in-law, Maura." She placed a hand on Autumn's shoulder. "You've already met Autumn."

They shook hands and completed the introductions, then a white-haired man wearing a gray suit and navy tie stepped out from the building. "I'd like an introduction as well, Hannah," he said, grinning. "And by the way, you did realize that other people were bringing food for the fellowship meal too, didn't you?"

"I just brought a few things," Hannah said with a shrug.

The man shook his head. "Your trunk was completely packed." He looked to Bo. "Took three people to help her unload it."

"Doesn't surprise me a bit," Hannah's father said, smiling with pride at his youngest daughter.

"I knew I had invited a few people to stay, and I always try to bring enough for at least another family or two. Plus I didn't want Jana to worry about cooking, so I told her I'd make enough for her also."

"*Told her* is right," Jana said. "She didn't give me a choice."

Hannah laughed and Autumn did, too, but Matt figured she didn't really understand the gist of the sisters' comments; she merely wanted to be included in the conversation, and he thought it was delightful. Not only was she conversing, but also interacting with others. This was truly a miracle.

"Well, I'm hoping that huge yellow Crock-Pot I saw them tote in had your chicken and dumplings inside?" the man asked.

"Wouldn't be a real church fellowship meal without them, now would it?" Hannah asked with a wink. "I used Mama's recipe, of course." She picked up a blue bucket from behind her on the sidewalk and moved up the stairs toward the man. Then she introduced Matt, Maura and Autumn to Brother Henry who, as Matt suspected, was the preacher. Ushering them into the building, she pointed out the auditorium, where the adult classes were held, and then indicated the hallway that led to Autumn's class.

"We're running a little behind, so I can let her walk to class with me, if y'all want to go on in the auditorium," Hannah said.

Matt squatted down to eye level with his little girl. "That okay with you, Autumn?"

His daughter's brown eyes were alive with excitement, with happiness, true happiness, and Matt's heart swelled at the vision.

"Yes, Daddy." She hugged him, the sweet smell of her shampoo enveloping him with her exuberant embrace. Matt swallowed, still relishing the sound of her saying his name and the sensation of seeing her happy again.

"Our room has fishing nets around the door. It's the only one that does, so it's pretty easy to spot," Hannah said to Matt. "Matter of fact, we're going to do a little fishing in class today." She indicated the blue bucket.

Autumn peered inside and laughed. "Cute fish," she said.

"Thanks, I made them myself." Hannah smiled at Matt.

She had an amazing smile, and he found himself tamping down on the desire to ask her to dinner or a movie, anything to spend more time together. But he hadn't lied to Maura earlier. He couldn't go through the risk of losing another woman he loved to cancer. Which meant he couldn't fall in love with Hannah Taylor.

"Anyway, if you want to come get Autumn after class and see how she's doing and all, our room is fairly easy to find." Hannah gave him a meaningful look, and Matt knew that she was trying to convey that he could come and see for himself whether Autumn would interact with the other children. She cared so much about his little girl.

"I'll find it," he promised.

Then he watched the two of them head down the class hallway side by side, before he and Maura went into the auditorium with Mitch, Jana and Bo to listen to Brother Henry's Bible study lesson.

Hannah's weekend had been wonderful, from working at the toy store with Autumn and Matt to having dinner at Mitch and Jana's and seeing those amazing ultrasound photos of baby Dee. Hannah had literally started crying when she saw the detailed images of her niece. She could see everything, Dee's eyes, her tiny nose, and her little fist, balled up against her chin while she sucked her thumb. She was already sucking her thumb! It was amazing, a miracle, for sure. She'd had a wonderful night with her family.

Today at church they'd share even more time together, and it would definitely be a lasting memory, because Bo Taylor was gracing a church pew again for the first time in over a decade. And Autumn Graham was getting a chance to make new friends in class.

Hannah stepped into the classroom with Autumn by her side. Maura obviously enjoyed dressing the little girl. Today she wore a crimson dress with a crisp black sash at the waist, white stockings and black leather Mary Jane shoes. Her shiny chocolate hair was pulled up in a high ponytail and topped with a crimson bow. The deep, rich color of the bow and dress seemed to make her eyes look even darker, her cheeks a little rosier.

The first time Hannah had seen the little girl, she'd thought she looked similar to the fancy porcelain dolls Mr. Feazell kept in the toy store's curio. But now Hannah thought she looked more like the American Girl dolls that were also on display in his store. The porcelain dolls were beautiful but didn't look as real, didn't actually show expression like the American Girl dolls. And Autumn had plenty of expression today.

She looked joyful.

"Everyone, this is Autumn," Hannah said cheerfully to the kids already seated at the table and coloring.

There were seven children seated, five boys and two girls, and all of them greeted Autumn before beginning a chorus of introducing themselves individually.

"I'm Daniel," one of the twins said.

"I'm Matthew," the other chimed in.

"I'm Shenae," one of the girls said with a giggle.

The other kids followed suit, either stating their name, or if they were too busy coloring, simply saying, "Hi."

Since Hannah had known she'd probably be arriving later than usual, she'd asked Jessica Martin to sit with the class until she got there. Jessica worked at a day care center in Claremont and was terrific with kids. Plus, her son Nathan was one of the most talkative, and subsequently one of the most enjoyable, kids in the class.

"I went ahead and gave them their coloring pages," Jessica said. "Here's one for you, Autumn." She placed the paper on the table in front of the chair next to Nathan's. "Nathan, did you introduce yourself to Autumn?"

Nathan had been so intent on coloring the boat on his paper that he hadn't seemed to notice Hannah's arrival. He'd joined in the whole group's welcome mumble, but hadn't personally greeted the newest visitor.

Hannah grinned. Nathan was dear to her heart because he absorbed everything she said each week and was the first to spout out what he had learned to Brother Henry after class. Then again, that may have had more to do with Brother Henry giving the boy a peppermint each time he listened to the lesson.

"Nathan, this is Autumn," Hannah said.

He looked up, those inquisitive eyes found Autumn, and he grinned. "Hey, it's you." His *s* had a bit of a slur due to lost teeth. Then he told Hannah with a shrug, "She knows me."

That got a small chuckle from Jessica. "Mr. Personality, that one," she said, running a hand over her son's sandy curls.

Hannah asked, "Do you know Nathan, Autumn?"

"He's in my class," she said. "At school. We're in Mrs. Johnson's class."

Nathan dropped his blue crayon, his eyes growing wide. "Mom, did you hear that?" His smile claimed his entire face and showcased three gaps from those lost teeth. "Wow! He must have said yes. I'm gonna have to tell Brother Henry." He gave her a crooked smile. "Might even get two peppermints."

Jessica shrugged and mouthed to Hannah, "I have no idea." Then she looked at her son, while Autumn sat in the chair next to Nathan and grabbed a pink crayon from the plastic box in the center of the table. "Nathan, you have to tell Brother Henry what, exactly?" Jessica asked.

"That God said yes. Don't you remember, Mom? I prayed to Him to let her talk, lots of words instead of a little bit, because sometimes—" he looked up at the ceiling and chewed on his lower lip while he tried to decide what to say "—sometimes Mrs. Johnson gets mad at her, not a whole lot mad, you know, but a little mad, I think. 'Cause she won't talk. But I knew she probably could talk more and maybe just needed God's help. Remember when we needed God's help for Daddy to find us?"

Jessica nodded, and blinked several times.

"So I asked Him to help her, and He must have said yes."

Hannah watched Jessica's mouth open in slight surprise. Nathan never failed to amaze them with his perception and with his incredibly kind heart. He'd led some of the most precious little boy prayers in Hannah's classroom that she'd ever heard, thanking God for everything from the fact that God brought him his daddy to the fact that his grandpa fixed the tree swing to the fact that he had a new little sister named Lainey.

"Nathan, that's wonderful and very thoughtful that you prayed for Autumn," Hannah said, having a time finding her own voice with his action deeply touching her soul.

"Brother Henry told me that sometimes He says no, sometimes He says yes. This time, He said yes." Nathan handed Autumn a blue crayon. "You should make your water blue. But you can make your boat pink if you want. I guess a boat could be pink, but I'm making my boat green."

Autumn took the crayon.

"You know my name?" Nathan asked.

Autumn smiled. "Nathan."

"Cool!" Nathan said, and of course, all of the other kids started asking Autumn if she knew their names, which took a few minutes, and Hannah walked to the door with Jessica.

"Thanks for watching the class," she said.

"You're welcome." Jessica looked at Autumn, repeating each name she was told, while Nathan smiled and nodded as though he had something to do with her entire speech process.

Then again, maybe he did.

"You have a special little boy there," Hannah said.

"I didn't realize she's the little girl he's been praying for each night. He said she's always sad." Jessica's brows lifted. "She looks happy now."

"I know," Hannah said. "Isn't it great when God says yes?"

Jessica laughed. "Yes, it is. I'm heading to class. Let me know anytime you want me to sub for you. This is a great group, isn't it?"

Hannah observed the kids, all chattering about their different-colored boats. And Autumn in the center of it all, smiling. "Yes, definitely a great group."

Jessica left the classroom, and Hannah sat at the end of the table and talked to the kids about their coloring pages, eventually making her way from marveling at their artistic talents to teaching them the Bible lesson, how Jesus asked Peter, Andrew, James and John to follow Him. The series of lessons for the fall revolved around Jesus teaching his disciples to be fishers of men, and Hannah truly enjoyed working the fishing theme into the lessons.

She tried to add something fun to the end of every Bible class, and today was no different. She'd told Mr. Feazell about her fall lesson theme, and he'd given her ten plastic toy fishing rods as yet another bonus to her regular pay. Hannah had tied a magnet to the end of each line and then had glued magnets to colorful, plastic fish for the kids to "catch." The fish were in a deep minnow bucket that Hannah had borrowed from her father, and each one had a Bible fisherman's name written on it, either *Peter, Andrew, James* or *John.* Hannah explained to the kids that the object of the game was to try to catch all four of the fishing apostles.

The game got a little loud, especially when the boys had their turns, with squeals, giggles, claps and shouts as each kid fished for a win. Nathan, who fished quite often with his father and grandfather, was determined that he would be the first to gather all four, but his first three attempts all yielded *Andrew.*

"I'm beginning to wonder if I even like Andrew," he mumbled on his fourth attempt, which sent Hannah, Autumn and the other two girls in the room into a fit of giggles.

Hannah and Autumn laughed so hard when he pulled out yet another *Andrew* that Hannah had laugh tears streaking down her cheeks and Autumn held a hand to her side.

And that's where Matt found them.

Brother Henry's Bible class had focused on a verse in Nahum about God being a refuge in times of struggle. More than once, Matt had met Maura's gaze, and he believed he knew what the smart woman was thinking. When they'd gone through the struggles of the last two years, they hadn't asked for God's help. In fact, they had actually turned from Him.

Now Matt was rethinking that decision, and he believed his mother-in-law was, too. His entire being felt startlingly at peace after the short lesson, and he looked forward to the main worship service, where he would have Autumn by his side for what he anticipated would be another meaningful, straight-to-the-heart lesson. God was speaking to him today, and Matt wanted his little girl beside him as it happened.

Walking to the classroom, he realized that he wanted someone else beside him, too. Hannah Taylor. Maura's comments before church had replayed in the back of his mind ever since, and more than once Matt found himself wondering what it would be like to have a woman in his life again. *No,* he corrected, he wasn't thinking about having a woman in his life. He was thinking about having Hannah Taylor in his life.

Truly she made him smile, not only because of her undeniable beauty, but with her genuineness and her love of life, her love of God, shining through. But he hadn't lied to Maura when he told her that he wouldn't pursue a relationship with the fascinating woman. The bottom line was that Hannah Taylor was in remission, and sometimes cancer came back.

Matt couldn't go through that again. Couldn't put Autumn through that possibility again.

With a heavy heart over that realization, he saw the fishnet-covered classroom door and stepped closer. Then, as quickly as his heart had been burdened, his spirits lifted at the vision before him: Hannah, wiping tears from her eyes, her full-bodied laughter ringing down the hall and blending with the giggles of his little girl, who hugged her gorgeous teacher and pointed at a blond-haired little boy whose evident frustration must have had something to do with a plastic red fish on the end of his line.

"I'm telling you, it's not funny," he said with a glare at all of the females in the room.

"Oh, Nathan," Hannah said, now moving a hand to her mouth as she laughed. "It really is." Which seemed to cause the laughter in the room to grow even louder.

A couple approached and peered in the doorway beside Matt. The man held a pretty toddler with curls so blond they were nearly white. She pointed to the frustrated boy.

"Bubba mad?"

The woman laughed. "No, Lainey, your brother isn't mad. Are you, Nathan?"

The boy tilted his head as though he had to think about it, but then forced a smile. "No, Mom, I'm not mad. I guess."

More laughter abounded, and Matt moved to the side as a few parents ushered in to pick up their kids and thanked Hannah for teaching the lesson.

Still wiping her tears, Hannah spoke to each family and made sure each child had their take-home papers before heading to "big church" for Brother Henry's lesson.

Autumn had moved to the blue fishing bucket and was rummaging through the plastic fish apparently searching for something. She withdrew a purple fish, then a yellow one, and continued searching.

"You ready, Autumn?" Matt asked.

"Not yet." She kept picking up fish, looking at them then putting them back in.

"Is Autumn your daughter?" Nathan's mother asked.

"Yes," Matt said, then added, "I'm Matt Graham."

"Nice to meet you," she answered. "I'm Jessica

Martin. This is my husband, Chad, and our daughter Lainey. And that, of course, is Nathan. He and Autumn are in the same class at school."

"Well, he seems like a very nice little boy."

"We're kind of prejudiced about that," her husband said with a grin, "but he really is."

Jessica Martin glanced at the kids then lowered her voice. "Nathan has been praying for Autumn every night, that she'll talk again. Well, that she'd talk more than a few words. That's what he has said in his prayers." She paused. "Maybe I shouldn't say anything, but he was very excited in class today when he heard her talking, and he said God answered his prayer with a yes. That's a big deal for Nathan." She smiled, and Matt's chest ached with gratefulness for the boy's kind gesture toward his little girl.

He swallowed, looked again at Nathan Martin, who Matt was determined to pray for before the day was over. It was time he prayed again, for sure. "I appreciate his prayers for Autumn," he said. "More than you could ever know. And the fact that God did indeed say yes."

Hannah looked up, evidently hearing Matt's comment, and she smiled. That smile, like the knowledge of Nathan's prayer, caused Matt's heart to squeeze. And Matt found himself staring into eyes that seemed to understand exactly what he felt, exactly what he wanted. Because right now what he wanted more than anything else was to feel whole again, with Autumn and with God. And even though he knew there was a risk, a big risk…perhaps even with Hannah Taylor.

"I found one!" Autumn exclaimed then she held

up an orange fish with *James* written on its side. She picked up the two fish she'd retrieved earlier and moved to Nathan. "Here, Nathan," she said, extending the three fish toward the still snarling boy.

His sandy brows drew down, green eyes squinted. "What's that?"

"Peter, James and John," she said. "Since all you got was a bunch of Andrew."

Jessica and Chad's laughter caused Nathan to give them a bit of a glare, but then he looked at Autumn and his toothless grin took over. He accepted the plastic fish with a somewhat embarrassed, "Thanks." Then he stuffed the four fish in his pockets, which was a bit difficult, but he managed, and told Autumn, "Isn't it cool when God says yes?"

Autumn nodded. "Yes."

"You need to get your fish," Nathan then instructed. "So you'll have something to play with in big church." Then he shot a look at his parents and added, "While you're listening to Brother Henry."

Chad and Jessica Martin were still laughing as they exited the classroom, and the remaining kids' parents all came and took their children, with each family making a point to introduce themselves to Matt and Autumn. Matt enjoyed the feeling of a church family, the way everyone knew each other and undeniably cared about each other. He had missed this portion of his life.

"Can we help you clean up?" he asked, watching Hannah gather up the extra coloring pages.

"You don't have to, but I never turn down help picking up," she said with a grin. She indicated the crayons, scattered around the tables like lengthy pieces of colorful confetti. "You can put the crayons in those plastic baskets if you want."

"I'll help you, Daddy," Autumn said.

"That'd be great." Matt dropped to his knees since the tables were kid-size and since he wanted to be closer to Autumn. "Is there a certain way we're supposed to do this?" he asked Hannah. "One color in each basket or anything like that?"

Hannah had finished gathering the coloring sheets and was beginning to untangle the fishing lines. "I usually try to make sure each basket has a few of each color. That way they're ready to go for the Wednesday night class."

"Gotcha." Matt and Autumn continued working together, her small hand brushing his occasionally as they placed crayons in the small plastic bins.

"This is fun, huh, Daddy?" she asked.

"Yes, honey, it sure is." They finished with the crayons, and he stacked the baskets on top of each other. "Where do they go now?"

Hannah was seated on the floor and still working on the fishing lines. She looked up, and one brown wave shifted into her right eye. Squinting, she blew it out of the way then grinned. "Anywhere on the shelf over there is fine."

"I'll put them up," Autumn said happily, and she shuffled the baskets to the shelves.

Matt moved toward Hannah. "Need a little help?"

She'd managed to untangle four of the lines, but the other six poles were still bound together in a knotted mess. "I wasn't thinking about how easily the fishing line would get tangled when I had them drop their poles back in the bucket. We didn't have to use all ten either, so I should have pulled the extra ones out, I suppose. Then maybe I wouldn't have all of this." She indicated the tangled mess.

"I believe it might work better if we take one of the magnets and work it back through." Matt reached for one of the tiny gray magnets then ran a thumb and forefinger along the clear line toward the thick knot until he determined which string to follow.

Hannah still worked on the largest knot, and Matt's fingers slid into hers as he slowly, gently pushed the magnet through. He noticed a slight tremble when their skin touched, then he looked up and didn't miss the way her cheeks had grown flush.

Matt swallowed, nodded toward the knot, the magnet in his hand, and the place where their hands now met. "I think sometimes it works best to take it one step at a time, instead of trying to work everything out at once."

Her eyes were dark, rich with emotion, and Matt wanted to ask her what she was feeling now, whether it was anything near what pulsed through him, the urge to hold her, to care for her, to really get to know the beauty of Hannah Taylor and let her continue to touch his heart, touch his soul.

"Did you hurt your eyes?" Autumn's voice broke through the moment, and Matt's little girl leaned her head over his shoulder to peer at Hannah.

Hannah blinked, looked from Matt to Autumn, and smiled, her cheeks once again tinged with color. "My eyes?"

Autumn nodded and leaned against Matt to point toward Hannah's eyes, or more precisely to the area below each eye, where smudges had formed from her earlier tears of laughter.

Matt hadn't even noticed, which made him even more aware of how fascinated he was by the woman in front of him. But now, thanks to Autumn's observance, he did see that Hannah's eye makeup had worked its way down toward her cheeks.

He grinned. "Your mascara," he said. "It's here." He ran a finger beneath one of his eyes to show her where.

Again, her cheeks flushed, and Matt was drawn to the beauty of her emotion, so easily seen in her expression. She rubbed beneath her eyes and smeared the dark smudge further.

Autumn giggled.

"Worse?" Hannah asked.

Autumn nodded. "But you're still pretty," she said, which caused Matt to chuckle.

"Here," he said, withdrawing a handkerchief from his pocket. "Let me help." He turned the soft fabric to place a corner in his grasp, then moved closer and gently rubbed the smudge away from the right eye, then the left. Tilting his head, he examined his handiwork and nodded. "All gone."

Autumn nodded too then moved to the other side of the room to get her take-home bag.

"She was right, though," Matt said quietly.

"Right?" Hannah asked, as the two of them stood, and she smoothed a hand across her bright floral skirt.

"Even with the smudges, you're still pretty." He absolutely loved the way those cheeks tinged with the slightest pink, and the way her throat gently pulsed as she swallowed through his compliment. "Very pretty," he added.

"I don't know what to say," she whispered.

"You can say thanks," he said, smiling, and really enjoying the fact that he found it so easy to smile around Hannah Taylor.

"It's time for big church now, right?" Autumn asked, moving toward them with her take-home bag in her hand. A red plastic fish, one of four, Matt assumed, stuck halfway out of the top of the brown paper sack.

Hannah glanced at the big round clock on her classroom wall. "Yes, it is time for big church," she said, a hint of embarrassment playing across her features. "We can go now."

Autumn started toward the door.

Matt turned to follow, but stopped when he heard his name.

"And Matt," Hannah said softly.

He turned back. "Yes?"

"Thanks."

Chapter Four

After the church service ended, Matt watched Hannah disappear with most of the other women in the congregation to prepare the food for a "dinner on the grounds." He'd enjoyed being around her in this atmosphere. Their moment in the classroom with the tangled fishing line was nothing short of magical. Sure, he'd mentally warned himself to control the attraction, because he couldn't risk growing attached to another woman with cancer. But he simply couldn't stop the desire to be with her, talk to her, laugh with her.

Seeing her interact with everyone at church only added to his impression that Hannah Taylor was something special. She was right at home in the congregation, chatting with the women around her and laughing as they discussed the abundance of food in the kitchen and the abundance of men chomping at the bit to get to it all. And the way she looked at her father throughout the morning, the happiness that beamed from her at seeing him in church, was breathtaking. But it wasn't her interactions with the church ladies or her happiness toward her father or even her delight toward Autumn's communication progress that touched Matt the most.

It was the way she looked at him. And the way she glanced away when he caught her looking. And the way she grew flush when he gave her a compliment. And the way she made him feel, as though he could survive anything, everything, with her by his side.

"Come on, Daddy, everyone's going outside," Autumn said, grabbing his hand and pulling him out of his reverie.

Maura stood a few feet away, her arms crossed and her eyes scrutinizing as she surveyed his expression. She saw him catch her gaze and winked, tilted her head knowingly and mouthed, "There's that look."

Matt shook his head at her but unfortunately felt his own embarrassment heating his cheeks, so he smiled, turned and walked outside with Autumn tugging his hand and Maura walking alongside them chuckling.

"Stop fighting it, William," she whispered.

"Wow, look at all the people," he said, ignoring her comment and instead marveling at the area bustling with excitement beside the church. He heard her laugh again and was glad to see Bo Taylor moving toward her and taking her attention off of Matt.

"Glad to see y'all are staying for the meal, too," Bo said. Then the two of them walked a few feet away and began discussing the worship service and the upcoming church activities for people their age.

Several members of the congregation made their way to Matt and Autumn, introduced themselves and welcomed them to the church. Matt had seen a few of them in his office or around town, but there was something different about introductions made at a church. People were friendlier, and definitely happier, almost as if they knew what a big step this was, for Matt to return to church and to bring Autumn and Maura back to God as well. He should have done this a long time ago, two years ago, in fact. It'd have been good for Autumn and Maura. And Matt.

The weather was perfect for the event, not overly hot and not too cold, simply a clear fall day that seemed made for an outdoor fellowship meal. Nathan wasted no time finding Autumn and taking her to the church playground, near the long assemblage of concrete picnic tables that were slowly but surely filling up with some of the best-smelling food Matt had been around in ages. Maura enjoyed cooking, but cooking for three didn't really lend itself to a lot of variety. Most of their dishes were one-pot meals, like spaghetti, chili, stew, or soup. The food laid out before him now was a smorgasbord of Southern hospitality.

Jana Gillespie, moving more in a side-to-side fashion than a steady walk, exited the side door of the church carrying a large casserole dish with two bright green potholders. Matt smiled at her and was always glad to see a breast cancer survivor doing so well, especially in her pregnancy. That'd been the primary question from most of his patients in Atlanta after hearing their prognosis. *Can I still have children?* Matt was glad that in most cases, he could tell them *yes*.

"Come on, I'll give you the lay of the land," Jana said to Matt as she passed him. "Because everybody has their favorites, so you'll need to kind of know what you're going for if you want the good stuff. Visitors get to go at the front of the line, you know, so you'll have an edge on your competition." She tilted her head toward her husband and a few other guys he stood beside near the table.

Jessica Martin walked closely behind Jana and had a basket of yeast rolls in one hand and a casserole dish in the other. She shot a look at her husband, standing next to Mitch Gillespie near the beginning of the tables. Chad Martin held their little girl and whispered in her ear as her mommy neared.

The toddler—Lainey, Matt recalled—pulled her butterfly pacifier from her mouth and laughed, then blew her mommy a kiss. Jessica blew one back. "Yes, visitors do go first," she said, pitching her voice toward the two men. "Although some people like to use, say, a toddler in their arms to convince people that they should have preferential treatment."

"Lainey's hungry," Chad said, "Aren't you, sweetie?" He bobbed his head with the question and naturally the toddler followed suit.

"Uh-huh, after all of the snacks she ate during the service, I think she can wait her turn." Jessica shot him an accusatory look. "Unlike some people I know. And you should be ashamed of trying to use your daughter for your own gain."

"Jess catches me every time," Chad said, laughing, and holding up one hand in surrender as he backed away from the table.

Mitch yelled toward his wife in an effort to defend his presence at the head of the line. "Jana, in case you're wondering, I was minding my own business and visiting with Chad. It just so happened that he was standing near the beginning of the line." He shrugged, grinned and looked guilty.

"Sure you were." She laughed and placed the steaming casserole dish on the table. "Why don't you two go check out the *end* of the line? There are quite a few new desserts this time."

"Your wife isn't fooling me," Chad said with a shrug. "She's moving us away from the plates."

"She isn't fooling me, either," Mitch said.

"But I guess it wouldn't hurt to go check out the desserts," Chad said.

"Okay, I'm game."

Chad nodded toward Jessica. "Besides, I'm sure she'd rat us out to Brother Henry anyway."

"That's right, I would. Now, go check out the new dessert Dorothy Collins brought. I heard her say something about blueberry yum-yum."

"Sounds like we need to investigate," Chad said.

"Can Lainey come and play with us?" Nathan yelled from the playground, and the blonde in Chad's arms squirmed and reached for the ground.

"Play," she said. "Peese?"

"Sure, but you keep an eye on your little sister," Chad said, putting the wiggling toddler down, then grinning as she ran toward Nathan, Autumn and several other children, all exerting pent-up energy they had accumulated from sitting through class and "big church."

Chad nodded toward Matt. "Come on, you can help us go check out this new dessert. Maybe Mrs. Collins will let us have a sample early."

"Matt's coming with me," Jana reminded. "I'm telling you, having a game plan for filling your plate is a priority here, and I need to help him out if he's going to compete with you guys."

"I'll catch up with you later," Matt said to the two men.

"Yeah, it's better to be smart and not mess with a pregnant woman when she issues an order, especially when she's my wife." Then Mitch lowered his voice and added, "But I'm fairly certain she wants to talk to you about more than the food. Just so you know." He smiled knowingly, and Matt found himself wondering what was really behind this "order" from Hannah's sister. Even so, he followed her directive and moved to stand beside her at the beginning of the chain of tables.

"All right," Jana said, "everything starts with the salads. We've got every kind of salad you can think of and probably a few you've never heard of. So here goes. This is the seven-layer salad, Mrs. Tingle's specialty, and it's amazing. Then there's the three-bean salad that Brother Henry's wife, Mary, makes. After that, there's broccoli salad, potato salad with onions and celery, and potato salad without onions and celery. That one depends on whether you like your potato salad crunchy or smooth. Then there's macaroni salad and sweet pea salad. Oh, and we have traditional green salad," she said, pointing to the one that looked the most familiar.

"Got it." Matt mentally pictured the seven-layer salad and potato salad—smooth, not crunchy—on his plate.

She grinned, and he noticed how her smile was almost identical to Hannah's, except for a dimple piercing each cheek. "Good deal." She stepped to the next section, but stopped her pace and moved her hand back to her belly. "Whoa." Her face tightened, and she appeared to hold her breath for a moment, then she exhaled.

"Just so you know, delivering babies isn't my specialty," Matt said, "but I'll do my best."

She laughed, but it seemed a bit forced, as though she might still be feeling a hint of that pain. "Braxton-Hicks contractions, false labor, or whatever you want to call it," she said, putting a hand on the table behind her and easing down, which caused her husband to jump into action and leave his new spot by the desserts.

"You okay?" Mitch asked, appearing instantly at his wife's side.

She waved him off. "I am perfectly fine. The doctor told us about these, remember?"

"Maybe we should go home and let you rest this afternoon," Mitch offered. "I could fix us a couple of plates to go."

She pointed a finger at him. "You'll do anything to be the first one at the food, won't you? Don't worry. I already stashed a few of Mrs. Jolaine's chicken fingers for you in the kitchen, in case they get gone before you get to them in line."

He smiled, then looked at Matt. "She knows the way to my heart."

"Right through his stomach," Jana said, then again waved him away. "Now I told you that I wanted a chance to talk to Matt in private. Go on, so I can do that before Hannah gets out here. She's still adding cracked pepper to those dumplings. She'll mess with them until they're 'Mama Taylor Perfect,' you know."

"Like I said, don't mess with a pregnant woman when she issues an order." Mitch kissed his wife then moved back toward Chad Martin, who was indeed sneaking a sample of something Matt presumed to be blueberry yum-yum from the dessert end of the line.

"You wanted to talk to me?" Matt asked.

Jana patted the place beside her on the concrete bench. "About my sister."

Feeling like a kid who'd been called to the teacher's desk, Matt took the designated spot. "About Hannah?"

Jana nodded.

"I'm listening." Matt found himself drawn to Jana Gillespie, in a way that said he could care for her, be a friend to her. She was very no-nonsense, very down-to-earth. Where he'd classify Hannah as beautiful or stunning, Jana would be cute or pretty. The fact that she was so far along in her pregnancy didn't take away from Jana's appearance. In fact, Matt would say it enhanced it. Her instinctive manner of protecting her unborn child, even now, cradling her stomach as though she could feel the tiny baby resting against her palms, touched Matt deeply. He imagined Hannah would be the same way when she was pregnant one day.

And there was something about the way Jana said Hannah's name, and the way she looked at her sister. The two were close, probably even closer than most sisters, which made sense. They'd been through a lot together, losing their mother, helping their father cope

with the loss and then suffering through their own bat-
tles with breast cancer together.

"I've prayed for Hannah to find someone who can
care for her, love her, the way Mitch loves me," Jana
said matter-of-factly. "I know the two of you have es-
sentially just met, but I can see these things. I mean, I
knew that Chad and Jessica were meant for each other.
I knew that Mitch and I were made for each other. I
even think I know who is meant for Daniel Brantley,
the man who is going to be our new youth minister.
But for now, I'll keep that a secret. Anyway, the point
is, I see love clearly. And I see it—Hannah and you."

Matt was taken aback by her directness. "Jana, I
think I know where you're heading, and…"

She held up a hand. "No, I don't think you do. I
might have this all wrong and maybe I'm not seeing
what I think I see when she mentions your name, or
when I see her look at you a certain way, or when I see
you looking at her." She paused then said, "During
church, you looked at her, at all of us, several times.
And I guess the only way to put it is that you were…"
She closed her eyes, apparently searching for the ap-
propriate word, then she opened them, and brown eyes
like Hannah's looked into his. "You were longing."

"Longing," Matt repeated, and felt sucker punched.
He *had* been longing, but he had no idea that he'd been
that obvious.

She nodded solidly, as though the word perfectly fit,
now that she'd thought of it. "Yes. You want what you
saw on that pew. You want what our family has."

"Which is…"

"Faith. Hope. And love. And, more than that, I'm pretty sure that you want it all with Hannah."

"Like you said earlier, your sister and I have only recently met, so it's a bit premature." Matt couldn't deny he'd thought something very similar during the church service, how amazing it would be to sit next to Hannah and know that she was a part of him, that he was a part of her, and that they shared something special, a faith, and a love. Yes, he'd basically just met her, but Maura had nailed it earlier. When he first met Rebecca, he'd felt something special. Something right. He'd known immediately that he could love her and looked forward to loving her for life. He hadn't felt that again until Hannah. But he also hadn't felt that horrid fear of potentially losing someone again until Hannah.

The subject of their current conversation exited the side door of the church with a huge yellow Crock-Pot grasped between her hands. Her eyes found her sister and saw Matt sitting next to Jana at the table. Then her brows knitted together in frustration.

Jana held up her hands as though she hadn't said a thing. "I've never been all that great at keeping my opinions to myself or keeping my mouth shut about those opinions," she said out of the corner of her mouth, as though she were trying her best as a ventriloquist. "Hannah knows that, and she probably even knows what we're talking about." She then gave an over-exaggerated smile to her sister. "Anyway, if the two of you do get close, and if you do end up falling in love with my sister, which I think you will, I want you to know that I think it's great. And personally, I don't think you should wait too long before asking her out.

She hasn't dated in quite a while because of her treatments. But she's not sick anymore, and I'm ready to see her live again."

Matt instantly recalled Maura's words from earlier. Maura wanted him to live again, and Jana wanted Hannah to live again.

"She'd be good for you, *great* for you. And she'd be wonderful for Autumn, too," Jana said, now forgoing her attempt to disguise the fact that she was speaking. But Matt stopped speaking altogether. He was too infatuated with the striking woman in the green sweater, floral skirt and shiny silver shoes carrying a wide yellow Crock-Pot directly toward them and looking at her sister as though she wanted to hurt her—badly.

"Jana?" Hannah questioned, setting the Crock-Pot on the table to the left of them. "Is everything okay?"

The scent of chicken and dumplings mingled with Hannah's sweet perfume, and Matt suddenly pictured her in a kitchen, an apron tied around her waist and Matt's arms wrapped around her while she cooked.

He blinked through the image. He had already made up his mind that he couldn't pursue a future with Hannah Taylor, but though his mind was made up, his heart begged to differ.

Jana's mouth stretched into her cheeks, dimples popping into place at once with the rapid transformation. "Everything's great!" She pointed down the table. "I was showing Matt the salads, but we didn't get to the rest of the food. Anyway, I'm going in to help bring out more casseroles. Why don't you show him all of the other things he can choose from, since he'll be at the head of the line and all?" She giggled. "Hey, if he fills his plate quicker, that means the rest of us will get to eat a little sooner, and I'm eating for two, you know."

Hannah's head tilted to the side. She wasn't buying Jana's explanation, but Matt wasn't about to tell her the real gist of his conversation with her sister. He watched Jana completely ignore Hannah's questioning gaze as she shuffled toward the church's side door. And when Hannah turned her accusing stare to Matt, he grinned. "So, you're going to show me what you've got besides salads?"

"That wasn't what you two were talking about," she said. "I'll find out eventually. I always do."

"Kind of figured you would," he said, which made her smile.

Have mercy, he liked that smile.

"It's a good thing I love her," Hannah muttered.

"I'm sure it is, because in her current condition, you could totally take her." Matt waited a beat and then got the exact response he'd wanted.

Her laughter rolled out and filled the air. "You're terrible."

He grinned. "Couldn't resist."

Still laughing, she waved her hand toward the abundance of tables that were becoming more and more jumbled with casserole dishes, Crock-Pots and platters. "Well, okay, since Jana gave me an order, I guess I better follow through."

Matt laughed. "Amazing how many people around here adhere to your sister's directives. Maybe I need her in the office instructing my patients."

"Probably wouldn't hurt," Hannah said, wiping her

eyes from laugh tears then looking at Matt. "More mascara problems?"

"Nope, it's pretty much all gone now."

"Super," she said, grinning. "So okay, she said you covered the salads, next comes the bread. Every kind of homemade yeast roll you can imagine, even sweet potato ones." She indicated a basket of rolls that held a hint of orange hue. "Those are actually pretty good. And we have cornbread muffins and cornbread sticks. Next are the sandwiches. You've got chicken salad, pimento cheese, egg salad, tuna salad and good ol' peanut butter and jelly ones for the kids."

"Autumn will go for the PB and J for sure."

"Most of the ones in my class do." She moved to the next section, and Matt listened as she told him about every kind of casserole and also indicated which sweet lady in the congregation prepared each one.

He liked being this close to her, chatting with her, listening to the sweet lilt of her voice, and hearing her laughter, always merely a short distance away and intermingled in her conversation. He now noticed that the sweet smell of her perfume held a hint of peaches and cinnamon, and when they reached the dessert area and she pointed out her famous peach delight, he assumed that was why.

A third man had joined Chad and Mitch, still hovering near the desserts, and Matt recalled him as the guy Brother Henry had introduced to the congregation as the new youth minister, who was due to begin working at the church full-time in the spring. He wondered if the guy, Daniel Brantley, had any idea that Jana had apparently already picked out his perfect match. The three men stood next to a lady currently handing the youth minister a square of something that looked, Matt presumed, to be the famed blueberry yum-yum.

Hannah cocked a brow at the trio. "What are you doing, exactly?" she asked, and then to the woman, "Mrs. Collins, you're spoiling them."

"They're good boys," the woman said then smiled at the three guilty guys.

"We were just trying to make Daniel feel more at home and wanted to offer him something special as the new youth minister," Chad said, grinning. "Mrs. Collins felt he should have a piece of her yum-yum as a celebration for his new job. Mitch and I hardly even tasted it." A dab of blueberry stuck to the corner of his mouth. Matt indicated his own mouth to show Chad he displayed evidence of his crime, and Chad quickly licked it away with a nod of appreciation to Matt for the heads-up.

Hannah shook her head, and Dorothy Collins laughed. "Well, I think it's terrible that you're already a bad influence on Daniel." Then she grinned at the newest member of the group. "But then again, if I remember right, Daniel Brantley was always sneaking desserts when he was younger, weren't you? Before he left for his years of world traveling."

"Hey, I was just trying to blend with my friends." Daniel licked some blueberry from his finger. "Besides, I've got another six months in Malawi before I start here full time. And they definitely don't have blueberry yum-yum there."

"Well, I guess I'll let you slide this time," Hannah said. Then she added, "I'm proud of you for all of your mission work, Daniel, but it is good to know you're coming back home."

"Good to be coming back."

Matt watched the interaction with admiration. Hannah easily brought her faith into the conversation. He respected the way that the small community kept up with its own and cared for its own, and he was at once appreciative to be a new part of such a close-knit group. And moreover, extremely appreciative to be a part of Hannah Taylor's world.

He watched her continue to chat with Mrs. Collins and the other men, while the remainder of the congregation slowly but surely moved toward the beginning of the table. Hannah was so striking, her smile contagious, her love of life shimmering around her like a golden light. Matt felt good simply being around her, and he had no doubt that Jana hadn't lied earlier when she said that she suspected Matt might fall in love with her sister. He could already tell that falling in love with Hannah Taylor wouldn't be all that hard. In fact, somewhere between the enormous array of salads and the blueberry yum-yum, he had made a decision. Or rather, two decisions.

One, he was going to tell Hannah Taylor the truth about who and what he was. And two, he was going to find his faith, forget his fears—and ask Hannah Taylor out on a date.

"Daddy, Nathan fixes his own plate. Can I?" Autumn stood beside the little blond boy, squinting up at Matt as they waited for his answer.

"Mama and Daddy watch so I don't get all desserts or all bread. They can watch her, too, if you want.

And I have to put something green on my plate. That's Mom's rule."

"That's a good rule, Nathan," Hannah said, while Matt laughed.

"Can I, Dad? GiGi can watch me do my plate, too."

"Sure," Matt said, then smiled as his little girl ran beside her new friend to the ever-growing line.

"Brother Henry is about to bless the food. We should get over there too if you want that coveted spot at the beginning of the line. You'll only qualify as a visitor for so long, you know." She paused, grinning at him, gold rays of sun sliced through the trees and into her hair.

"I think I'll let someone else have the front spot this time," he said.

"Really? Why?" she asked. "Like I said, this visitor thing will only last for so long."

"Because I need to tell you something."

"Tell me something?" Her dark eyes widened. "About what?"

"About me, about my past. You may have noticed that Maura slips from time to time and calls me by the wrong name."

"She's called you William," Hannah said. "I wondered if maybe she had a son named William, but I didn't really know her well enough to ask."

"She doesn't have a son named William," Matt said. "She's calling me by the name I went by before, in Atlanta."

"You were called William?" Confusion apparent on her expression, she seemed to realize that this conversation was more intense than she'd first anticipated.

She stepped a little farther away from the bustle of commotion around the tables, more toward the towering oak trees that bordered the church grounds. The leaves were starting to turn, with small bursts of yellow and gold mingled with the green. Hannah leaned against the trunk of one of the largest trees and waited for Matt's explanation. "Should I be nervous about why you would have changed your name?"

"Well, I haven't done anything illegal, if that's what you're thinking," he said, glad that she was making this less difficult for him, her eyes filled with understanding already, even though she didn't know the reasoning behind the change.

"Witness protection program, right?" she asked teasingly.

"Afraid not," he said. "Nothing that glamorous."

"Okay," she said, smiling and nodding at a family that passed by them with full plates on their way to a picnic table. "I don't have any more guesses, but first things first. What is your real name?"

He cleared his throat. "My full name is William Matthew Graham, and I went by William before, when I worked in Atlanta."

"So Matt is a shortened version of your name," she said, apparently eased by this revelation.

"Yes, of my middle name."

"But you started going by Matt because…"

He ran a hand through his hair, glanced to see if anyone was near enough to hear and decided that they were alone. "You knew that I was a doctor in Atlanta."

"Yes."

"And I was, but I wasn't a general physician. I actually worked at a research facility and was considered something of a specialist in my field. I had a notable success rate," he said, "but we called it survival rate." He waited for the words to sink in.

"*Survival* rate," Hannah repeated, and he saw the moment that realization dawned, when she glanced down at the tiny pin on her sweater. "You knew a lot about Jana's tests during the pregnancy and about the risks of her being pregnant if her cancer returned."

His eyes also focused on her pink ribbon pin. "I worked with advanced experimental research at the Atlanta Breast Cancer Research Center."

Chapter Five

Hannah's mind struggled to process what Matt—or William—said. Her doctors were in Birmingham for the most part, but she'd heard about the research center in Atlanta and had even considered going there for treatment if she hadn't finally been deemed cancer-free last year. The Atlanta Breast Cancer Research Center was one of the most notable centers in the country, with the absolute best doctors and analysts working toward finding a cure for the disease. Hannah's oncologist in Birmingham often mentioned medical instruction that he'd received from his affiliation with the renowned center. And Hannah had prayed for the doctors there, specifically for the research teams that were trying new techniques to combat the dreadful disease that had so thoroughly impacted her family.

In other words, she'd prayed for Matt before she even knew him. But he'd left the center, and as the pieces fell into place, she thought she knew why. "When did you stop working there?"

"Two years ago." His jaw tensed, and he nodded

toward more people that moved past them on their way to find a place to eat.

Hannah knew he was getting a grip on his emotions, and she didn't want to press too much. He'd left after his wife died of the very disease he was trying to cure. Now he was opening up to her about something very difficult, and she was grateful that he could trust her enough to tell her the truth about the pain of his past. She found that she couldn't be around Matt Graham without wanting to know more about him, wanting to be more a part of his world, and right now, she glimpsed a part of him that she suspected he'd kept hidden since he lost his wife.

Thank you, God, for letting him trust me. And thank you, God, for bringing him here, to Claremont, and to me.

She waited patiently while he kept his eyes averted, not quite ready to tell more, but eventually he looked back at her, and Hannah saw the vivid sorrow in their depths. He cleared his throat. "We worked with the most severe cases, the ones that had been deemed without hope, given less than a year to live."

Hannah nodded, remembering the day that the doctors had told her family that they should enjoy what time they had left with her mother.

"And I was blessed to have a better than ninety percent survival rate with my advanced stage patients. It was the best record at the center, the best in the country, in fact." His head subtly shook as he spoke. "I've never handled losing a patient well, but ten percent was the best record out there, and I dealt with it okay, until…"

Autumn and Nathan passed by a few feet away, and Autumn held up her plate for his inspection. "I did good, Daddy!"

He swallowed, gave her a smile. "Yes, you sure did."

"Look, Miss Hannah!" she said, showing her plate.

"She's got green beans. That's her green thing," Nathan said.

"Yes, she does." Hannah pushed past the array of emotions overwhelming her so she could speak to the kids. "Good job, Autumn."

"My green thing's fried okra," Nathan said, indicating the vegetable on one side of his plate. "Mama says I'll eat anything that's fried. She says that means I'm Southern. But I really do like the fried okra. Hey, we're going to sit at the kid table, okay?"

"Sounds good," Matt said then turned back to Hannah, dabbing discreetly at her eyes. He noticed. "I'm sorry I upset you."

"It hurts to realize what you've been through," she said. "You could handle that you weren't able to save a hundred percent, until your wife was in that ten percent."

He nodded. "And then...then I couldn't face the thought of losing someone else. I couldn't go back to the research, to the gamble, if I couldn't even save Rebecca."

Hannah looked away from the crowd and finished brushing away her tears. "I'm so sorry."

"I knew when I moved here that people might be interested in my background, want to look up my physician's records and all. It's human nature. I thought perhaps if I changed my name that it might lessen the chance of someone realizing that my specialty was in treating breast cancer and I could start over as a general practitioner."

"The newspaper article said you practiced medicine in Atlanta, and I guess everyone was like me, assuming you were a general practitioner there, too, that we were lucky to get someone in Claremont with experience in a bigger city."

Matt smiled. "I'm glad that was enough for everyone here. Plus, there are over twenty doctors named Matt Graham or Matthew Graham in Atlanta and the surrounding areas, so even if they did search the internet for me, they'd probably have thought I was one of those."

Hannah and Matt nodded or spoke to a few members of the congregation as they passed with full plates. Jana and Mitch neared them, Mitch's plate piled to a nearly unmanageable mound.

"Dude, you missed your chance at the beginning of the line, and now Mrs. Jolaine's chicken fingers are long gone."

"That's okay," Matt said. "I was planning on the chicken and dumplings being my main course."

"Hate to be the bearer of bad news," Mitch said, popping a deviled egg in his mouth, "but I think I could see the bottom of that Crock-Pot when I dipped mine out."

"That's okay," Jana said. "I'm pretty sure Hannah has more warming on the stovetop, don't you, Hannah?"

"Wouldn't be smart not to bring plenty," Hannah said. She waited for a lull in the traffic then lowered her voice. "I appreciate you telling me your past, especially since I'm sure it's painful talking about losing Rebecca."

"It didn't seem right, not telling you."

"Well, it means the world to me." She smiled at Brother Henry as he and his wife walked by.

"Y'all better go get some food, before Chad, Mitch and Daniel head back for seconds," the preacher instructed.

Hannah moistened her mouth, nodded. "Yes, sir, we will." The intensity of their conversation had almost made her forget that they were still at the church fellowship meal and that they were probably drawing attention since practically everyone else had fixed their plates. "I'm going to get the rest of the dumplings, then I'll meet you at the beginning of the line."

"Hannah, wait," Matt said, catching her wrist as she turned to go.

His palm was warm against her skin, and the eagerness of his words caused her to step toward him with the touch of his hand.

"Yes?" she asked, her gaze drawn to the point where his palm encircled her wrist.

"I—I haven't dated since Rebecca…" His voice dropped off, and he closed his eyes.

Hannah had never wanted to help anyone more than she wanted to help Matt Graham now. She'd never wanted to hold anyone more than she wanted to hold him, right here, right now. But they were standing directly in the center of the entire church membership, and it didn't seem the right place or time for the embrace tugging at her heart, so she simply said, "Matt."

He opened his eyes, gave her a slight smile. "This is a little more difficult than I remember."

"Do you want to ask me something?" she asked softly. "Because I think the answer is yes."

He nodded, and it touched her that a man this successful, this amazingly handsome, seemed a bit nervous about asking her out. "Yes," he said, his mouth lifting at the corners. "I definitely want to ask you something."

"Okay," she said. "Ask."

He cleared his throat. "Would you like to go with me to the First Friday celebration? As my date?" he asked, and Hannah found herself fighting a laugh when his voice actually cracked in the middle of the question.

She placed her hand on top of his, still encircling her wrist. "I can't think of anything I'd rather do."

Chapter Six

A patient's late arrival Monday afternoon put Matt about a half hour behind the time he normally left his office and consequently caused him to miss meeting Autumn and Maura when they got to the toy store. Worse, he hadn't been able to get there a little early, which had been his original plan, to see Hannah.

He needed to talk to her again, because the more he'd thought about their conversation from yesterday, the more he realized that he still hadn't told her everything. Sure, he'd told her about his past at the research center and that he'd given up his role on the research team after Rebecca's death, but he hadn't explained that asking Hannah out on a date wasn't merely difficult because he hadn't asked anyone in a very long time. It was difficult because she was a survivor, and because he didn't want to risk losing someone again.

He exited the building, started toward his car and wondered whether it was wrong to withhold that deep-seated fear from Hannah. Was there any reason to tell her? As Maura had continued to remind him, Hannah's remission should keep him worry-free. But there was that niggling fear at the back of his mind that reminded him of the truth.

Sometimes, cancer comes back.

Matt climbed into his car and thought of Hannah, her laugh, her smile, her eyes. "Everything is going to be fine," he said, tossing his bag onto the opposite seat and withdrawing his phone from his pocket. He'd missed three calls from Maura while he was in with his last patient, and he wanted to make sure everything was okay.

The phone rang twice before Maura picked up.

"Hello, William," she answered. "How are you?"

"I'm fine. How's Autumn? Is everything okay?"

"I believe she had a good day at school. We just got to the town square. The carpool line took a little longer than usual today, and her teacher wanted to chat for a moment. Do you want us to wait for you before we go into the toy store?"

"No, I'm sure she's eager to see Hannah. I'm already in the car, so I'll be there soon."

"All right. Then can you hold on a second? We're nearly there."

"Sure," Matt said, listening to the familiar noises of the town square, geese squawking, people chatting, and then the recognizable bell on Mr. Feazell's door.

He heard Hannah's greeting to his daughter and couldn't hold back a smile at knowing they were together again, particularly when he heard Autumn's enthusiastic, "I can't wait to get started!"

"She's excited, huh?" he asked Maura through the phone.

"I'd say." Maura told Hannah that she needed to

finish her conversation with Matt before coming into the display area.

The bell on the door sounded again, and Matt knew his mother-in-law had stepped outside, which also meant that whatever she was going to say probably wasn't anything she wanted overheard. He braced himself.

"Okay," Maura said, her voice lowered. "I need to tell you the rest. I asked Autumn how her day was."

"And?"

"She said 'okay.' And then nothing else until we got here."

Matt had hoped that Autumn would completely break out of her shell, but it'd been the same this weekend, she had barely talked at all except when necessary, but then she'd been fine at church around Hannah. So he could handle this. He could. She would get better, eventually. It'd just take time, and faith, and prayer. Matt had prayed today more than he'd prayed the entire time since he'd lost Rebecca, and it'd felt good, very good, to talk to God again.

"Thanks, Maura."

"I wish I had better news."

"I know," he said, and he did. Maura loved her granddaughter as much as she'd loved Rebecca, and she wanted her to heal as much as Matt did. Unfortunately, Matt didn't think Maura would ever completely recover from losing her daughter until Autumn was completely okay.

"William?"

"Yes?"

"Her teacher asked again whether we had considered holding Autumn back another year. She said that it might give her time to start communicating with the other…"

Matt interrupted her before he could hear the rest of the teacher's recommendation. "Autumn doesn't need to be held back again. She's six years old, and she'll be seven in June, well before the next school year starts. And she's excelled in everything academically this year in first grade. Why should she go through it again merely because she isn't speaking all the time? It isn't her brain that's the problem. It's her heart."

Maura's deep sigh penetrated the line. "We'll figure out what's best for her, I have to believe that, but I agree that holding her back isn't the answer. She's doing so much better, with Hannah."

An image of Autumn, her arms wrapped around Hannah's legs outside of the church building, flashed across his mind. "Yes, she is."

"They're talking and laughing now," Maura said. "Oh, I told the teacher that she should call you and talk to you because you could let her know about Autumn's progress. She doesn't know, because she hasn't seen this." Maura's soft chuckle came through the phone. "I'm watching them through the window. Hannah has another bag of those treats from the Sweet Stop, and right now the two of them are holding licorice under their noses making candy moustaches." She paused a beat then said, "She's so good for Autumn."

Matt nodded. "I agree."

"I'll stay until you get here, then I need to get home and finish dinner. I'm trying one of the casserole recipes that I got yesterday at the fellowship meal."

"Sounds good."

"It isn't only Autumn, you know," Maura added. "Hannah's good for you too. I'm glad you asked her out."

"I didn't tell you that I asked her out."

"You did, though, didn't you?" Maura asked.

He laughed. "Yes, I did, to First Friday."

"Good for you," she said. "Okay, they're calling me back in. See you in a little while." She disconnected.

In no time at all, Matt was at the town square walking toward the toy store. Through the shop's window, he saw Hannah and Autumn huddled over a dollhouse and working intently on putting up something that looked like a red curtain against the dollhouse wall. Maura leaned forward on the visitor bench so she could get a better look. She said something, and Hannah and Autumn both turned to her and laughed.

Hannah must have caught a glimpse of him as he neared, because she turned, still laughing, to look at Matt. Then she waved, tapped Autumn and pointed to Matt. He could easily read Hannah's lips. *"Look who's here."*

And he could also read Autumn's squeal. *"Daddy!"*

He waved then proceeded through the entrance and toward the display. As soon as he pulled back the curtain and stepped inside, Autumn started filling him in.

"Miss Hannah says we need to do the photography store today, and that store has a fancy red cloth hanging up." She crawled toward the window and pointed to the photo shop that centered the left side of the square. "See?"

"Yes, I see," Matt said, nodding a hello to Hannah.

She wore a fitted red sweater, jeans and sparkly ballet slippers, these in bright red sequins. And naturally, her pink ribbon pin was tacked on the top of her sweater. Matt found himself as drawn to the way she studied him as he was to Hannah herself. She didn't merely look at him, she took him in, her eyes focusing on his face, then his pullover and khakis, then back to his face. Oddly, he had that same type of feeling as a guy showing up for a first date, where you're wondering if you picked the right thing to wear and if you'd say the right thing when you spoke. Matt hadn't felt that self-conscious since he was a teen. But he did now. And something about that realization made him feel very much alive.

"It's time for you to live again." Maura's words from Sunday echoed in his mind, and he grinned. He was living again, thanks to Hannah.

"How has your day been?" he asked Hannah.

"Great, and yours?"

"Just got better."

She ran her teeth across her lower lip and then grinned, clearly taken aback at his honesty. But Matt was telling the truth. His day had something missing until this very moment, and that something was Hannah Taylor.

She reached past him to get a small box of miniature photographs. "I'm looking forward to Friday," she whispered as her mouth neared his ear.

"Me, too."

"Daddy, GiGi thought this was a sewing store because of the red cloth," Autumn said, indicating the fabric that she and Hannah had placed in the tiny shop's window. "But really it's the dropback for the photo shop."

"The backdrop," Hannah corrected with a grin. "But that was close."

Maura straightened. "Well, after I looked at the real photo shop, it was obvious. But I just saw a bunch of red fabric and assumed they were decorating a sewing store."

Autumn laughed. "A sewing store. You're funny, GiGi."

"Actually," Hannah said, "Diane Marsh has a shop that has a fairly large sewing section. Her place is mostly filled with crafts, but she does have a nice area for those who like to sew." She leaned toward the window and indicated a colorful store near the candy shop. "That's it. Scraps and Crafts. All kinds of crafts plus scrapbooking supplies. We have a lot of people around here that really get into scrapbooking. In fact, a group meets at our church every Tuesday night to scrapbook, and Diane comes in to teach the ins and outs. She does a great job, from what they say."

"Really," Maura said. "Well now, I've never been much for sewing, but I've often wished I knew how to scrapbook. I've saved every photo and most all of the artwork Autumn has done. It'd be nice to display that in a scrapbook. What time do the ladies meet at the church?"

Hannah laughed. "They meet at six every Tuesday night, but it isn't only ladies. I'll have you know that my dad signed up for the class yesterday when he came to church."

"Bo?" Maura asked, obviously surprised. "He's wanting to scrapbook?"

"Well, I should probably clarify. Jana told him he needed to get out more, and she said she wanted to have a nice scrapbook started for baby Dee but she knew she wouldn't be able to fit the class into her schedule after the baby comes. Then she waltzed him over to the sign-up bulletin board at church, and..."

"She signed him up," Maura said with a laugh.

"Yeah, but he didn't take his name off the list, so I think he's going to do it."

Maura nodded. "Well, that's good. And that settles it. I'm going, and I'll have a friend in the class."

Hannah grinned, and so did Matt. Looked like he wasn't the only one giving "living again" another shot. Maura and Bo Taylor were also venturing into new worlds, starting with the world of scrapbooking.

"Well, I'm going to head home to start that chicken and rice casserole." Maura stood from her seat, took a step then stopped. "Autumn?" she asked, her voice raised a little.

"Yes?" Autumn held a tiny framed photo in each hand as she looked up. "What, GiGi?"

"You had a paper in your book bag that said this Wednesday is your I'm-the-star day at school. Is that right?"

"Yes, ma'am. I can bring in one favorite thing to talk about, as long as it fits in a brown paper bag and isn't alive."

Hannah laughed. "That sounds good. Maybe Mr. Feazell would let you take one of the miniature items from our display and you can tell how you're helping me create the town square for the toy store's window."

"That'd be great!"

"And the paper also said that you have illustrated a book that you'll share during story time."

Autumn nodded. "I'll show the pictures to the class."

"And tell about the book?" Maura asked. She was working hard not to appear too interested in Autumn's answer to her question. But Matt wasn't fooled.

Autumn didn't answer, but nodded. Matt looked at Hannah, both of them realizing the problem with this scenario. Autumn would have no problem showing the pictures to the class, but if she wasn't speaking except when Hannah was around, there wasn't any way for her to tell about the book.

"Autumn?" Hannah asked.

"Yes?"

"Would it be okay if I came to the story time part on Wednesday and listened to you tell about the book?"

Autumn's face lit up, then fell. "I'm not sure."

"You're not sure?" Matt asked.

"I think only parents, or maybe grandparents, can come. That's all that have come to see other kids."

"When is story time?" he asked.

"It's at noon," Maura said, "according to the schedule they sent home. They do story time right before lunch."

"That's right," Autumn said.

"Well, that's perfect for me," he said. "I can take my lunch break, grab something quick to eat and then be there for story time. And if she still wants to go, I can bring Miss Hannah with me."

Hannah smiled at him. "I would love to go," she said.

"Great!" Matt said, echoing with Autumn's "Yay!" from the floor.

Maura nodded. "I think that's a marvelous idea," she said. "And I feel fairly certain that this will be a story time that Mrs. Johnson will never forget."

Chapter Seven

Bo Taylor walked toward the Young at Heart room at the church with even more apprehension than he'd felt Sunday morning when he'd entered the lobby upstairs. The last time he'd attended church regularly, he and his wife Dee had been a part of the Middle Marrieds group. Now he'd shot straight into the senior citizens bunch, and he wasn't sure it was an accurate placement. Was forty-nine really that old? Okay, fifty in a month, but still…he sure didn't feel senior-ish.

Probably to save electricity, the primary hallway lights were off and small wall lights were placed sporadically along the path to the oversize room. But there was no denying which room would be seeing all of the action tonight. The beam at the end of the hallway burst into his path like a scene from *The Twilight Zone*. And Bo had the same eerie feeling, like the hall kept getting longer and longer, his goal farther and farther away.

He contemplated turning around and heading back to the world where he was comfortable, back at home sitting in his favorite easy chair scanning ESPN for all things football. But he'd promised Jana that he'd give this a go, and he sure hated disappointing his girls. However, he anticipated stepping into that bright light and seeing a bunch of sweet older ladies who'd wonder what in the world he'd been thinking when he signed up for that scrapbooking class.

What *had* he been thinking?

"Promise me, Daddy. You need to try new things, meet new people. It'll be good for you," Jana had said as she guided him to that sign-up board on Sunday. Bo had peered at the choices. Scrapbooking had seemed the lesser of two evils, since the only other new activity starting this week was quilting. Like that was going to happen.

He should have told Jana that he'd just wait until they started a fishing group. Or golfing. No, he'd never golfed a day in his life, but he'd bet it'd make him feel a lot more manly than scrapbooking.

Bo blew out a breath. *All right, God, if this is where I'm supposed to be now, I want You to help me be happy about it. Please,* he added, stepping into the glaring light then squinting while his eyes adjusted to the difference.

He'd anticipated four or five extremely elderly women to be sitting at the tables with a bunch of ancient shoeboxes filled with worn photos that they deemed scrapbook worthy. But there were at least forty people seated in the room. And while there were quite a few silver-haired ladies in the bunch, there were just as many silver-haired males. And the room also held brunette ladies and blondes…and one auburn-haired lady who looked up from her spot at a table and smiled.

Thank you, God.

"Bo! Come on over," Maura said. "I saved you a spot next to me. I hope that's okay." She indicated the chair beside hers at a table filled with several of Bo's friends from around town.

He walked to the table, grinned at the group and then directly at Maura. "How'd you know I'd be here?"

"Hannah told me. I hope you don't mind that I signed up too. I've been wanting something to do with my time, and when she said that you were going to give scrapbooking a go, I thought it'd be nice to do something with a friend."

Her words warmed him to the core, and made him smile again. Have mercy, it felt good to smile.

"I don't mind at all," he said.

Maura smiled broader. "Wonderful." Then she looked to the rest of the folks seated around the table. "This is Mae Martin. Her son is Chad, who is little Nathan's father. And this is Bryant and Anna Bowman. They're Jessica's parents," Maura said, obviously excited to introduce Bo to her new friends. He let her continue the introductions, but exchanged glances with all of his buddies around the table. He didn't want to embarrass Maura by telling her they'd all known each other for most of their lives. Apparently, her life in Atlanta didn't lend itself to a culture where everyone knew everyone in town. And she seemed to be having so much fun, well, Bo didn't want to ruin it.

Unfortunately, Maddie Farmer, intently working on organizing the scrapbooking items surrounding her at the table, didn't get the drift that everyone was trying to be polite and let Maura do introductions. When

Maura got to the nurse, Maddie laughed. "Oh, goodness, we've all known Bo for years," she said with a
wave of a marker-filled hand.

Maura's flushed cheeks said she realized her error,
and Bo wondered if she'd be hurt that he hadn't told
her sooner. But then she laughed, a beautiful sound,
and shook her head. "What am I thinking?"

"You're thinking that you've met new friends,
and you wanted me to meet them too," Bo said, still
touched by her action. "And I appreciate that, even if
there's nothing new about this brood for me. They're
all old as dirt, since they now qualify for the Young at
Heart class. But then again, so do I."

That caused a lot of rumble at the table, but for the
most part, they all laughed and agreed. Or told Bo that
he was the only one resembling dirt.

Then Diane Marsh, the instructor of the class and
owner of Scraps and Crafts, cleared her throat and welcomed them all to Scrapbooking 101.

For the next hour, Bo got an introduction to albums,
themes, stamps, die cutters, stencils and stickers. Bo
attempted to concentrate on the terms and the supplies
scattered around their table, but that was more difficult when sitting beside Maura. She was so absorbed
in everything Diane described and so obviously happy
to be included with the group that he found himself
entranced with her enthusiasm. And with her, period.
Their visit at the town square fountain had introduced
him to a new friendship with someone who'd also had
some rough circumstances in life. Then their continued conversations on Sunday at the church dinner had
told him that she was easy to talk to, fun to be around.

But this, tonight, had been a welcome surprise, that she'd considered him a friend and someone she actually wanted to spend time with, scrapbooking of all things.

She reached for a pair of bizarre-looking scissors from the center of the table, picked up a piece of bright turquoise paper and cut around the edges, creating a wavy border. Bo watched her hands turn the square of paper, noticed her nails were painted a shiny pale pink and that there was something very delicate about the way she manipulated the blue square.

Suddenly, her hands stopped and he realized that her attention had turned from the paper in her hand to him. "You aren't enjoying this, are you?"

He blinked, realized that he'd been so enthralled with watching her that he hadn't paid attention to the fact that the square-cutting was a group activity. Everyone else at the table, everyone else in the room, in fact, had also picked up a paper and started to cut wavy-edged borders. "Actually," he said, attempting to lower his voice as much as possible, "I'm enjoying this very much. I just got so carried away with watching you work that I forgot to do my own."

Honest was the only way Bo knew how to be. Dee had always claimed him to be honest to a fault, but she'd also said that was the main thing she loved about him. Evidently, Maura appreciated it as well, because she smiled at him so tenderly that his heart warmed at the sight.

"Bo Taylor, I believe that's one of the sweetest things anyone has ever said to me," she whispered back.

"Well, it's true," he said, on a roll now, and quite

happy that Bryant Martin was chatting so loudly with his wife that he didn't decide to rag his friend for getting mushy at the scrapbook table. Bo picked up a piece of red paper and started cutting as well. "There's no way I can get my hands to move the way yours do," he said. "That's what had my attention. It's so, well, graceful, I guess you'd say."

She'd been cutting more waves when he spoke, but her hands stopped, and she looked directly at Bo. "I used to hear that often, when I was young, but it's been a long time," she said softly. Then she cleared her throat and explained, "I was a dancer when I was young."

Maura's words were spoken at a lull in the table's conversation, and Maddie Farmer jumped on her statement.

"You danced? What kind of dancing?" she asked.

Maura shrugged, a bit embarrassed, but said, "Ballet. Not professionally or anything, but I danced throughout my school years. I loved it."

"Why did you stop?" Anna Bowman asked.

Maura smiled. "I married when I was nineteen and then had my daughter at twenty-one. Then I simply enjoyed being with her, watching her dance and play and enjoy life. Dancing took a backseat to other things." Her voice faded as she added, "I always thought I'd like to dance again, though."

"Well, it isn't ballet, but there is a ballroom dancing class starting up at the Stockville Community College next month. Several of the other nurses at the hospital have been talking about it. I'd thought about giving it a try and can give you the information about it, if you'd like."

Maura's face lit up, and Bo could almost see her in a big room, music playing and her smile beaming as she danced. "I'd like that very much," she said. "Thanks."

"No problem," Maddie said, then turned in her chair to peer toward the front of the room, where Diane Marsh held up a completed scrapbook album and discussed themes.

Maura's attention had returned to her hands, and Bo knew she was thinking about his words. He leaned toward her and repeated, "Very graceful," then smiled.

"Thank you." The emotion in her words was undeniable, and Bo was again thankful for his tendency to always say what was on his mind. Who'd have thought that telling this pretty lady that her hands were graceful would so obviously touch her heart? But it had, and Bo was very grateful for the opportunity to make Maura smile.

"Hey, Bo, here's a topic that we're more familiar with," Bryant said, nodding toward the word Diane Marsh had written on the dry erase board.

Bo looked toward the front of the classroom, where Diane drew a line under the word *Tools*.

Bryant had been subtly poking fun at the scrapbooking instruction all night, but Bo hadn't missed the fact that Bryant had already withdrawn several photos of his grandson Nathan from his wallet and had made notes on a pad that included a list of potential themes. *T-ball, Preschool* and *Kindergarten* headed the list.

"I'm betting scrapbooking tools don't include table saws," Bo replied to his friend.

Before Bryant could answer, Maura said, "According to this supply list, the tools include punches, paper trimmers, templates and embossers." Then she leaned forward and picked up a small football-shaped wood cutout from the sample scrapbooking items Diane had placed in the center of their table. "But I'm betting you could make these types of embellishments with a jigsaw or a coping saw, don't you think?"

Bo's jaw dropped, and Maura noticed.

She laughed. "What, you don't think females know anything about tools?"

He honestly had to think about that question before he answered, "Well, until a second ago, I didn't."

That caused quite a round of laughter at the table that was so loud that they ended up apologizing to the surrounding tables.

Maura's laughter finally subsided and she explained, "My father was a carpenter." She shrugged. "I enjoyed spending time with him, but he was always in his shop. So I figured the best way to get time with my dad was to learn about his work."

"You ever help him build things?" Bo asked.

"Sometimes," she answered, and her face reflected the happiness of a distant memory. "Nothing huge or anything, but he'd let me hold the wood, taught me how to drive a nail and also taught me a thing or two about tools."

"But not punches, paper trimmers or embossers?" Anna Bowman asked teasingly as she held up the list of scrapbooking supplies.

Maura laughed. "No, I still have a lot to learn about all of those."

The group continued chatting and enjoying each other's company until Diane ended the night with a discussion of digital cameras. Realizing his own camera was woefully outdated, Bo took a few notes on that subject and decided he'd shop for a new one soon. He'd need a decent camera to take photos of baby Dee soon.

After the class ended, Bo, Maura and the rest of the group moved to the tables Diane had set up along the side walls that displayed sample scrapbook albums. The themes were endless. Bo found a "Baby's First Year" scrapbook and flipped through the pages, marveling at the way the book told a story. The first page displayed a young couple in various stages of hugging and kissing with captions about "Celebrating the wonderful news" and "Children are a heritage from the Lord."

The next pages were filled with photos of ultrasounds that became more and more detailed as the pages progressed, and then the birth announcement, along with the hospital form where two tiny feet had been stamped on the page. Another page had a small bracelet with pink beads that spelled out *Emma.*

Bo felt his throat thicken. "I believe I still have both of the girls' bracelets like this. They gave them to all of the babies at Claremont Hospital back then."

Maura stood beside him and nodded. "I still have Rebecca's, too. She was born at the Dekalb Medical Center near Atlanta."

Bo flipped through the remaining pages in the album. "My girls need something like this. We saved pictures, and things like that, but nothing has been organized before. This—this would mean a lot to Jana and Hannah."

Maura nodded. "Well, now that we've started our class, you'll know what to do to put it together, right?"

He smiled. "I'll do the new baby's book right. Go ahead and start at the beginning and make sure she has something special for every memory."

Maura moved to the next book, titled Kindergarten Memories. "I've saved everything Autumn has ever made," she admitted, "so I'm thinking I can make a good go at saving all of those memories, too." Her hands moved delicately across the embellished pages of the kindergarten-themed album and again, Bo was mesmerized by the gracefulness.

"You should dance again," he said.

She stopped looking at the album and turned dark eyes toward Bo. "You think so?"

He nodded. "Maddie said they have that ballroom dancing class starting at the community college soon."

"Yes," she said, then waited while Bo got up his nerve.

"I'm thinking ballroom dancing probably is a little easier if you have a partner," he said.

Her smile gave him all the encouragement he needed.

"And I'm thinking I'd like to give it a try, too, if you're up to spending time together beyond scrapbooking, that is." Bo hadn't felt this surge of confidence in years, that excited feeling when you ask a girl out and you absolutely, positively know without a doubt that she'll say yes.

And Maura didn't disappoint.

"I definitely think I'm up to it," she said, grinning.

Bo felt like a teen again, and it was an amazingly good feeling. In fact, the one-word response that came to mind was *awesome,* but he reigned in that reply and answered, "That's great."

Chapter Eight

Hannah pulled into the Claremont Elementary parking lot at a quarter before noon on Wednesday and wondered if her apprehension was more because she was attempting to help Autumn talk in front of her teacher, or because she was spending more time with Matt. She'd seen him every day since they met, and she found that she looked forward to the moment when she'd see him each day. They hadn't even been on an official date yet, but he already felt like a part of her life. A very important part of her life.

She parked next to his black BMW, went inside and signed the office registry, then walked to the first grade hall to find Matt standing outside of a classroom. Each class had a felt flag embellished with some type of animal hanging beside the door. The door where Matt stood had a blue flag with a green frog and the words *Mrs. Johnson's Jumping Frogs* on the fabric flag.

He wore a blue-and-white-striped button-down and navy pants. His arms were folded and his jaw tense. It didn't take Hannah but one glance to know that something he saw in that classroom bothered him terribly.

She moved to stand beside him under the frog flag and saw that he was peering through the skinny glass window that composed the right half of the door. The children were inside, gathered at different tables around the room and working on various activities.

Matt looked at her, his face definitely grim. "She's over there." He pointed to the table against the far wall, where Autumn and three other children worked on some sort of magnetic ball puzzle. "They're doing centers."

"You didn't want to go inside?" Hannah asked quietly.

"I wanted to watch a little first, see how she was interacting, since the teacher has had a problem with it and all."

"And?"

"Watch."

Hannah stepped closer to him so they could both have a good view of Autumn's table, where the other three children chatted about something or other, probably how they were going to make their set of magnetic balls look like the finished picture example hanging above the center, and Autumn merely watched. She still used the small set of silver balls in front of her to try to help them accomplish the goal, which was good, but her mouth never moved, remaining in a set flat line while the others all appeared to be unaware of her standoffish behavior. "Bless her heart."

"I know. They aren't even trying to talk to her, because they assume she won't respond, and they're okay with that," Matt said thickly.

Hannah looked up at him and saw that he could

barely contain his tears. "They just don't want to hurt her feelings," she said. "I bet they tried to communicate with her for a while before they stopped. They probably don't want to embarrass her." It could be worse, Hannah realized, because the children could have gone another route and made fun of Autumn's peculiar behavior. She started to tell Matt, but decided that probably wasn't what he wanted to hear. His little girl was having a problem, and as a result, he was hurting.

God, please help her come out of her shell with us here. Let her come back to him completely, Lord, and if it be Your will, please let it be today.

Hannah opened her eyes and peered back through the glass. "Matt, look," she said, keeping her tone low but excited.

Nathan, carrying a big bag of what appeared to be building blocks, moved to Autumn's table and said something to her. The teacher stood behind him as he waited for Autumn to look up, smile and nod. Then Autumn grabbed one handle of the bag and Nathan held the other, while Mrs. Johnson went to the back door of the classroom and held it open for the pair to cross through.

"That's a good boy," Matt said, his words filled with emotion.

"Yes, he is," Hannah said, and she added a silent thank you for Nathan Martin to her prayer.

Matt moved his fist to the door. "Well, here goes."

"God is here," Hannah said. "He'll be with us, and with Autumn."

Matt's concerned face converted to a smile. "You know what? I believe you." He turned toward her. "I'm glad He's here, and I'm glad you're here, with me. It will mean a lot to Autumn, and it means a lot to me."

The door opened, and a little black-haired boy with dark eyes stood before them. "I'm Ryan," he said, showcasing a gap where a front tooth used to be. "I'm the door opener today."

"Well, thank you for opening the door, Ryan. You're doing a great job," Hannah said. "We're here for story time."

The little boy's head tilted. "You Autumn's parents?"

Mrs. Johnson looked up from where she was at the back of the classroom and smiled, while Matt answered, "I'm Autumn's father, and this is mine and Autumn's friend, Miss Taylor."

Hannah smiled, and wondered if it was normal the amount of pleasure she had for that fleeting moment while the little boy assumed she was Autumn's mommy.

"Hello, I'm so glad you could come," Mrs. Johnson said, her words directed toward them as she wove through the children still cleaning up from the centers. "Autumn hadn't said anything about anyone coming, so I had assumed she would be doing her story on her own. I mean, well, she hasn't said much of anything, so I guess that doesn't sound quite right. Anyway, I asked her yesterday if she had anyone coming to story time, and she said maybe."

Matt nodded.

"Now, we all understand Autumn's situation," Mrs. Johnson continued, "so I thought I could ask her to hold up her book to show the pictures she illustrated, and then I will make up a story that goes with those pictures."

"I thought it was a story the children came up with," Matt said.

"Well, it is. But, you know, this exercise involves the children merely illustrating their individual stories and telling us the words that match the pictures to form the tale. See, most first graders aren't at the point where they can write a story in full sentences. They're still learning their sight words and all. So this helps them feel a sense of accomplishment by letting them basically author a story without having to write all of the words. They draw the pictures and then tell us the story." She paused, sighed. "So with Autumn, I thought I would tell the story."

"Can we let Autumn tell her own story?" Matt asked.

"Why, yes, of course. I mean, I always ask if Autumn would like to verbally demonstrate her thoughts and feelings, but as I've mentioned on the phone, she simply isn't that developed in her communication skills." Another pause. "And as I mentioned to her grandmother yesterday, if that continues, I think it'd be best for Autumn to perhaps repeat first grade, but we can decide more about that as the year progresses."

Matt's mouth clamped closed, and Hannah's heart ached for him.

Stay with us, Lord, she prayed. "We can let her try to tell her story first, though, right?" Hannah asked. "In case she does decide to communicate verbally today?"

Mrs. Johnson's smile was instant and almost a little too perfected. "Of course."

"Thank you," Matt said curtly.

"Now both of you can go ahead and sit in our story time corner, over there," Mrs. Johnson said, indicating an area at the front left of the classroom that was covered in pictures of books and characters and had lots of colored squares lined in a semicircle around a center seat. "The parent chairs are on the right."

Sure enough, there were a few adult-size chairs on the right side of the circle, obviously set up so that the parents could sit directly behind all of the children and view their own child in the spotlight.

"Thank you," Hannah said, taking Matt's arm and leading him to their parent chairs. She sat down, waited for him to sit beside her. "This is nice."

"She isn't," Matt grumbled, eyeing Mrs. Johnson, gathering the children up and telling them it was nearly time to hear Autumn's story and then go to lunch.

"I'm sure she means well," Hannah offered, but she'd also been less than thrilled with Mrs. Johnson's assessment of Autumn's behavior.

"You're too nice," he said. "Way too nice." Hannah smothered her laugh.

"Now, class, as soon as Autumn and Nathan return from taking the blocks to Mrs. Dade's room, we'll listen to Autumn's story and then we'll head to lunch. Make sure if you brought your lunch that you already have your lunch bag or lunch box at your table place and ready to go. If you need lunch money or milk money, put that in your pocket now."

The kids scurried to follow instructions, and then one by one, came to sit in the semicircle and wait.

"Now remember, we are quiet when our friend tells her story, because everyone's story is important," Mrs. Johnson instructed, and the bounty of heads accumulating in the circle bobbed in agreement.

Matt and Hannah waited while they eventually all sat down. Finally the back door opened and Nathan came through with Autumn following close behind.

"Hey, Miss Hannah!" Nathan exclaimed, which caused Autumn's head to pop up and her face to break into a face-splitting smile. The two hurried through the classroom, and Nathan plopped down on an open purple square. "I'm glad you came for Autumn's story," he said.

"I'm glad, too," Autumn said.

Hannah heard more than saw Mrs. Johnson's gasp, but she definitely saw Matt's face grin with pride.

"Hello, princess," he said, while Autumn moved into his arms for a big hug.

"Hello, Daddy."

Hannah looked toward the teacher to see her hand over her mouth, her eyes wide with surprise.

"So, you're going to tell us your story?" Hannah asked Autumn.

"Yes," she said, beaming. She gave Hannah a long hug and then turned and moved to the center of the circle, where all of the other children waited to hear what Autumn Graham had to say.

Thank you, God.

Mrs. Johnson seemed to collect her bearings, blinked a few times, and then said, "Okay, class. We're going to be very good listeners while Autumn tells her story." Then, to Matt and Hannah, "Each child could write a story about whatever they chose, either about something that has happened to them, like a trip they went on or a gift they received, or about their lives in general, or even a favorite pet. Whatever they choose to tell about," she explained, her voice a little choppy from the apparent surprise of seeing Autumn speak for the first time.

Matt and Hannah nodded, with Matt's smile never wavering as he glowed with pride toward his little girl.

Autumn smiled at her teacher, then at her classmates, and finally at Matt and Hannah, then she withdrew an oversize fabric book from an easel and said, "My story, by Autumn Graham."

Hannah looked at Nathan, squirming on his square and telling every child around him, "See, I told you she can talk."

"Nathan, we need to *quietly* listen," Mrs. Johnson warned.

"Yes, ma'am," Nathan said, then looked at Autumn and grinned. "Just happy 'cause God said yes."

Mrs. Johnson nodded, though Hannah was certain she didn't understand the impact of what the precious little boy had said, but Autumn giggled a little, and Hannah was thrilled that Nathan had managed to break the tension of her first spoken sentences in the classroom.

"Okay, go ahead, Autumn," Mrs. Johnson said. "We're all listening." She motioned for Nathan to turn around and sit down, which he did.

"My story," Autumn said, turning the page.

The first picture was filled with tall skinny buildings or houses, and three stick people standing off to one side.

"This is my daddy," Autumn said, pointing to the tallest of the three, with a patch of black hair and a smile. The bodies weren't more than a straight line with more lines forming arms and legs and a circle for the heads, but each circle had a face, and all three faces had big smiles. "And this is my mommy." She indicated the next figure, again smiling, with lots of red curly hair. "And this is me." The smallest figure, also smiling, with brown hair past its shoulder. "This is when we lived in Atlanta and I stayed with Mommy and Daddy went to work."

Hannah noticed Matt's smile waver a bit, but he nodded his approval at his daughter.

Autumn turned the page. There were three figures again, but the three were different than before. Two were the same size, basically, and then there was the little one that depicted Autumn. There were some squiggly lines and circles around them and tall trees. "This is GiGi. She's my grandmother. She's my mommy's mommy. And when Mommy got sick, GiGi came to live with us, and Daddy stayed at work. This is when we went to the park. We went to the park a lot 'cause it made Mommy feel better to be outside and watch me play."

Hannah's hand moved instinctively to find Matt's, and she squeezed it gently, knowing that this was tough for him. He didn't look at her, and she thought she knew why, because if he looked at her, he might let go of the sadness that was probably at the brink of being set free.

Autumn smiled at the group and held the book out so that they all could see the picture. Then she turned the page, and three figures were on the page, one lying down on a straight line that Hannah assumed was a bed. "This is me and GiGi. We are taking care of Mommy while Daddy works."

Hannah examined the picture. There were several things that were different, but two obvious ones stood out immediately. Autumn's mommy no longer had her pretty red curls, and instead a colored hat, kind of flat like maybe a scarf, circled her head. And Autumn's face had no smile. In fact, she had no mouth at all. And one more thing Hannah noticed, drawn on the mommy's chest was a little pink swirl. A pink ribbon.

Hannah noticed the look of pity in Mrs. Johnson's face. The children all listened intently, none of them seeming to realize the emotional dilemma behind Autumn's story.

Another turn of the page depicted three figures, and thankfully, the daddy was included again. "This is my daddy and me and GiGi, when we moved here, to Alabama." The daddy looked the same as before, tall with black hair. GiGi also looked the same. And Autumn's small figure still had one primary feature missing. Her mouth.

Matt's palm was warm against Hannah's and she continued holding tight to him, hoping that somehow she could give him the strength he'd obviously need to get through this. There seemed to be one more page in the story, and Hannah prayed that it'd be better than the other ones on Matt's heart.

Autumn turned the page, and there were four figures now. "This is Daddy, and GiGi, and me—" Autumn looked up at Hannah and Matt "—and Miss Hannah." Thankfully, Autumn's figure now had a smile, wider than any of the previous smiles, and Hannah's heart soared. "I'm very happy here. We're all happy here." She held the book out and moved it in a half circle around her to let the children see the picture.

Mrs. Johnson cleared her throat, and Hannah was fairly certain she saw the woman brush her fingers beneath her eyes. "Autumn, that was a lovely story, and we truly appreciate you telling it to us. Don't we, boys and girls?"

The group clapped and emitted a chorus of "Yes!" and "Good job!" to Autumn.

"Okay, now, class, you can all gather to get your lunch items and line up at the door. Nathan, you're our line leader today, so please go stand by the door, and everyone get your quiet faces on before we walk down the hall."

The boys and girls quickly gathered their things and began lining up behind Nathan, while Autumn walked over to Hannah and Matt and hugged them.

"Did you like it?" she asked.

Matt swallowed. "Very much. I'm proud of you, angel. Very, very proud."

"Thanks. Did you like it, Miss Hannah?"

"Oh, yes, Autumn."

Matt appeared to notice that all of the children had

lined up except Autumn, and he cleared his throat, then motioned for Mrs. Johnson to come over.

"Yes, Dr. Graham?" the teacher asked.

"Would it be okay if we brought Autumn to the lunchroom? I'd like to spend a few minutes with her, if that's all right, to let her know what all we liked about her story."

The woman's eyes warmed, and she smiled tenderly at Autumn. "I think that's a wonderful idea." She paused then added, "And Dr. Graham, I believe I was wrong earlier, when I thought I knew what was best, you know, for next year. I can see that with the correct approach, everything will be right on track, and I promise to help make that happen."

Hannah was so grateful for the woman's words, because she and Matt both obviously knew what she was saying, that she wouldn't try to hold Autumn back. Autumn's communication wasn't the problem here; it was more than that. And Hannah had a feeling that Matt was going to try to figure things out right here and now.

Help him, God, to say the right things to Autumn. And please God, help this wonderful little girl to find her way out of her shell for good. Help her live again, because I truly believe that's what Matt needs too, and Maura, to see Autumn complete again. In Your Son's precious holy name, amen.

"We'll see you in the lunchroom, Autumn," Mrs. Johnson said.

Autumn, now sitting in her daddy's lap, nodded. "Yes, ma'am."

Matt waited for the line of children to leave then

glanced behind him to make sure they were the only ones in the room. They were. "Autumn," he said, "that was a very nice story. You're really a good little artist, did you know that?"

She had the book in her hands, and she nodded. She opened it to the first page. "Did you know that was you?" She pointed to the daddy on the page. "Before I said it was?"

"I had a strong suspicion," he said with a soft laugh.

"All of the pictures are very nice," Hannah added. "I love the colors that you chose."

"Thanks," Autumn said, her pride evident in the single word.

Matt casually flipped through the pages, and Hannah held her breath, wondering how he was going to approach the huge issues displayed on the fabric. "On this one," he said, showing the first page where he was missing, "you said that I was at work, right?"

Autumn nodded.

"You know," he said, "I'm not sure if you realized it back then, but when I went to work, I was trying to help Mommy get better, too, like you and GiGi were doing at home. I wanted her better, and I wish that I could have stayed with all of you while I was trying to do that, because I didn't like being away from you so much."

"I didn't like being away from you so much either," Autumn said softly.

Matt swallowed, kissed his little girl's forehead and turned the page. "And here, when Mommy was sick," he said, showing the one where Rebecca's image was lying on the bed, "I think you forgot part of your picture here."

Autumn squinted her face, her little mouth moving to the side as she examined each item on the page. "What?"

"Your mouth," he said, smiling. "There isn't a mouth on your picture."

"I could get a crayon so you can draw one in," Hannah offered.

Autumn shook her head. "No, there isn't a mouth."

Again, Matt visibly swallowed, breathed in deeply, let it out. "How come, sweetie?"

"Because I stopped talking."

Matt didn't seem to know what to say, so Hannah asked, "Why did you stop talking?"

This time, Autumn looked up and tears filled her dark eyes. "I don't know. I got scared, because Mommy kept getting sicker and sicker, and Daddy wasn't there, and I didn't know what to do. So I stopped talking. And then, then Mommy got sicker and then she went to Heaven. Because I stopped talking."

"Oh, honey," Matt said, releasing Hannah's hand and stroking his daughter's hair. "Mommy didn't go to Heaven because you stopped talking. Mommy went to Heaven because she was sick, and because God wanted her to go on to Heaven so He could make her better." He squeezed her against him. "You—you started talking again when you saw Miss Hannah," he reminded.

"Because she's like Mommy," Autumn said. "I saw her ribbon, and I knew. And I have to talk, or she'll go to Heaven, too."

The impact of her words was like a fist squeezing

Hannah's heart. "Oh, sweetie, I love it that you talk to me, but I am better. You don't need to worry about that."

"But—I love you," Autumn said.

"I love you too," Hannah said, meaning every word. "And I'm glad that you wanted to talk to me, that you wanted to keep me from getting sicker, too." Hannah struggled for the right words. Thankfully, Matt took over.

"Precious, I'm so sorry. I had no idea that you thought Mommy got sicker because you stopped talking. That wasn't it, baby. I promise. God was just ready for your mommy to go to Heaven, and He's taking good care of her there. She didn't go away because you stopped talking. It was because she was so sick that no doctor could make her better." He kissed her head. "Do you understand, precious? It was not your fault."

"And Autumn, you don't have to talk around me just to keep me from getting sick again," Hannah said. "But I would hope that you would talk around me anyway, because I love listening to you talk. And you know what?"

"What?" Autumn said, a small smile playing at the corners of her mouth.

"Everyone else likes listening to you talk, too. Did you see all of those boys and girls listening to your story? They liked hearing you talk, too, especially Nathan."

"He's my friend," Autumn acknowledged.

"He's a very good friend," Hannah said. "And I think it'd mean a lot to him, to Mrs. Johnson and everyone if you would talk whenever you wanted, like you used to, before your mommy got sick. It makes people happy when they hear you talk."

"And it has nothing to do with whether someone is sick or not, whether you talk to them," Matt said. "All of that is up to God. And He has His reasons for taking some people to Heaven early. Obviously, He knew your mommy was special and wanted to take good care of her when she got so sick."

"Nathan says that sometimes God says no, and sometimes God says yes," Autumn said.

Matt laughed. "Yes, and we all know that Nathan is a smart boy."

"So we're okay to talk again, to everyone?" Hannah asked.

"I guess so," Autumn whispered.

"Okay, well, go get your lunch things," Matt said, "and we'll walk you to the cafeteria."

Autumn moved to a cubby with her name on it and withdrew a pink Barbie lunchbox from her backpack. Then the three of them walked to the cafeteria, with Autumn pointing out the classroom flags that she liked best along the way.

Matt and Hannah waited until she was seated near Nathan and several other children, then they said goodbye to Autumn, her classmates and Mrs. Johnson before heading back toward the exit.

Outside, they walked to their cars before saying a word. Then Matt leaned against the side of his, placed his hand at the bridge of his nose then spread his fingers across his eyes. "That was nearly more than I could take. I'm—very grateful that you were here with me."

"I'm grateful, too. God had a reason for us coming

to story time today. He wanted you to know what was locking her inside, and He wanted to help us find a way to set her free again."

"I prayed about it," he admitted.

"I did too," she said with a smile. "And sometimes, God says yes."

Matt laughed at that then he reached for Hannah and drew her into his embrace. "Thank you, thank you, thank you, God…for saying yes."

Hannah found herself pressed against him, and she noticed that he didn't release her. In fact, he held her there, close against him. Then, while her heart raced so prominently she was certain he could feel it, Matt gently placed a finger at her temple then brushed it along her cheek, down her jaw, sending a trickle of excitement across her skin with his touch. He eased it beneath her chin, then gently tilted her face toward his. "We're still going on that date Friday?" he asked, his words feathering across her lips.

"Yes," she whispered, losing herself in his clear blue eyes.

He edged his mouth even closer to hers, then kissed her sweetly, tenderly, until Hannah nearly forgot that they were in the school parking lot. Nearly, that is, until the loud brakes of a garbage truck screeched through the parking lot, and Matt ended the kiss with a laugh.

"Thank you," she said, and then, when he laughed again, she was embarrassed that she'd just thanked him for a kiss. She grinned. "Sorry, I guess I'm out of practice."

"Actually, I wanted to thank *you,* Hannah."

Her mind raced. Why was he thanking her? "For helping Autumn?"

He gave her another brief kiss that left her lips tingling. Then he smiled. "For saying yes."

Chapter Nine

Hannah couldn't miss the difference in Maura when she brought Autumn to the toy store Wednesday afternoon. Obviously in high spirits, she smiled ear to ear and laughed as they entered the display area.

"I hear story time today was a big hit," she said. "Autumn *told me* all about it on the ride over!"

Autumn grinned shyly, and Hannah knew exactly why Maura seemed so joyful. She was communicating with her granddaughter again, really communicating. "GiGi's excited," Autumn said, looking at her grandmother.

"Well, it was a very special story time," Hannah said.

"I started to come." Maura sat on the visitor's bench. "But I didn't know if me being there might, well, mess things up."

Autumn shook her head. "You could've come, GiGi. All parents and grandparents can come." She looked at Hannah. "And very special people can come too."

Hannah winked at her. "Thanks."

Maura smiled even wider. "I know, honey, and you better believe me, next time, I'll be there with bells on."

"Bells?" Autumn asked. "What kind of bells?"

Maura tossed a hand to her chest and laughed. "Not real bells, sweetie. It's a saying. It means I can't wait for the next story time."

Autumn nodded. "Oh." Then she turned toward Hannah. "Daddy called us after we left school. He was finishing up at work, but he said he'll be here soon."

Hannah grinned. He'd called her, too, told her he'd be late and also told her how much today had meant to him. "I'm glad." And truly, she was. She couldn't wait to see Matt again. She'd worked on the dollhouses all afternoon, but her mind had been on one thing: that amazing kiss. Well, two things. Autumn shining in front of everyone in that classroom and finally telling Matt and Hannah why she'd stopped talking for so long *and* that amazing kiss.

Maura still seemed unable to control her smile as she fiddled with the furry scarf around her neck and gazed at her granddaughter with undeniable adoration. Meanwhile, Autumn had already started entertaining herself by resituating the tiny geese they'd put around the fountain and making hysterical squawking noises in an attempt to mimic the noisy birds.

"Oh, Autumn, you're too funny," Maura said.

Autumn grinned. "You be this one, GiGi." She held up the biggest of the birds, and Maura didn't bat an eye before starting a squawk that outdid all of Autumn's attempts. Autumn couldn't keep up her own end of the noisy banter; she was too lost in laughing at her grandmother.

Hannah was thrilled to see Maura like this, happiness practically spilling over. She was even dressed cheerfully this afternoon. Every other time Hannah had seen the lady, she'd worn typical fall colors, dark maroon, forest green, deep gold. All were pretty, of course, but not nearly as vivid as the cheery red top she wore today that she complemented with that fun multicolored scarf. Even her makeup looked a little brighter, with a bit of champagne sparkle on her brows, a hint of blush on her cheeks and a rosy red lipstick that exactly matched her blouse.

"I love your outfit," Hannah finally said when she figured it was obvious she was staring. "You look so, well, happy."

"I *am* happy," Maura said, laughing, and she leaned forward and ran a hand down Autumn's long curls. "For the first time in years, I am very, very happy."

"Me, too!" Autumn said, which made Maura laugh even more.

The curtain shifted, and Matt stepped through grinning at all of them. "I attempted to wave to you through the window, but you were all too busy laughing to notice."

"Sorry about that," Hannah said, grinning, because like Autumn and Maura, she was also happier than she'd been in a very long time, and all because of the man looking at her now.

"Don't apologize," he said, blue eyes finding hers and holding her gaze. "It's perfect."

"I agree," Maura said, still stroking Autumn's curls. "It is perfect, absolutely perfect." Then something caught her attention and she looked out the display window and grinned. "There's Bo."

Hannah turned to see her father, smiling, and walking toward the store. He saw them looking and held up something small and silver for them to see. "What's he got?" Hannah asked.

"Oh, he bought one!" Maura said. "He told me that he'd get one for our scrapbooking class, but I didn't know it'd be this soon."

"Get what?" Hannah asked, but Maura didn't have to answer. Bo Taylor had already entered the store and pulled back the curtain.

"Everybody look natural," he said, holding the silver camera out and then snapping a photo. "I'm still getting used to the features, but this thing is amazing. Isn't it something how far they've come since the girls were little? I had no idea."

"Bo wanted a nice camera to take photos for our scrapbooking class," Maura explained. "That one looks great. I need to get a new one, too."

"I talked to Mandy Carter over at the photography shop to see what she recommended," Bo said. "She suggested this—" he held up the camera again "—and I love it. I can take you to look at the different models and see what you like," he offered. "This one comes in pink, but I didn't think that was my best color."

Maura laughed. "That sounds great. I'd love to shop for one. So, what all can this one do?"

Matt looked at the two of them, checking out Bo's camera, then glanced at Hannah and grinned.

Hannah smiled, too. Apparently last night's scrapbooking class had been a huge success, not only with the scrapbooking, but also in developing Maura and Bo's friendship.

"I thought we could go over to Diane Marsh's store today and check out those supplies she was talking about last night in class," Bo said to Maura.

"I'd like that," she said, standing, and again fiddling with her scarf. "I wanted to see those new three-dimensional stickers she talked about."

"Yeah, me too. I'm pretty sure I saw some track stickers, and both of my girls ran track in high school. I'll need some of those."

Hannah blinked. "You're doing scrapbooks for me and Jana? For our high school years?" Her father had taken lots of photos back then, and he'd rarely missed one of their track meets. But there had always been an underlying sadness to everything they accomplished because of their mother's absence.

His hands gripped the camera, and he gave Hannah an apologetic look. "I didn't do anything like that back then, but those years were important. I mean, I saw some of the sample scrapbooks there at the class last night, and well, you and Jana did a lot in school. You should have something special like that to show for it. I thought I'd work on that for your Christmas presents, if that's okay."

Hannah was certain her mother would have probably done scrapbooks for them if she'd have still been alive at the time, but Hannah had never thought anything about not having one. Now though, the fact that her dad thought of the sweet sentiment and was planning to do something so special touched her immensely. "It's definitely okay, Daddy."

"Well, I can't take total credit. Maura saw those high school examples last night and asked if you and Jana had anything like that. After I realized you didn't, I decided to make an effort to remedy that. And Maura offered to help me." He looked at Maura. "Thanks again."

"You're welcome." Maura smiled at him, then at Hannah. "He was going to try to surprise you both for Christmas, but then we realized that he'll have to get a lot of the photos and such from you two, so there was no way to keep it a total secret..."

"But you can't actually see it until Christmas," Bo completed. "So that will be the surprise part."

Hannah was seated on the floor to work on the display, but she stood, moved to her father and hugged him. "Thank you, Daddy."

He patted her back. "Well then, Maura and I have to get over to Scraps and Crafts before they close and let Diane show us the new stuff."

"I'm ready," Maura said then looked to Matt. "I'll see you at home in a little bit. Dinner is ready, and I hope you don't mind, I asked Bo if he wanted to eat with us before church. We are going to the Wednesday service tonight, aren't we?"

"Of course, and that's fine for Bo to come over for dinner," Matt said.

"Hannah, we'd love for you to come, too," Maura said. "I made plenty. We're having Mrs. Jolaine's chicken fingers, Maddie Farmer's broccoli salad and Mrs. Collins' blueberry yum-yum for dessert."

Hannah laughed. "When did you get all of those recipes from the church ladies?"

"Last night at our scrapbooking class," Maura said. "So, will you come to dinner?"

"Sure," Hannah said. "It sounds great."

Autumn looked up from playing with the geese. "Miss Hannah, will you be my teacher again tonight at church?"

"I sure will. And we'll be learning some more about those fishermen in the Bible."

"Maybe Nathan will catch more fish tonight," Autumn said. "I'll say a prayer for that." She closed her eyes, and her lips moved slightly for a few moments, then she opened them again. "Okay, now we'll just need to see if God said yes."

"That's right," Hannah said, while Matt chuckled.

Bo slid the curtain aside for Maura then paused. "Hannah, did you ever hear back from the doctor?" he asked.

"No," she said. "But I forgot to call and ask, too."

His brows furrowed a little. "Will you call today?"

"Yes, I will, in just a minute. And I'm sure everything is fine."

He nodded. "Well, let me know what you learn."

"I will, Daddy."

"We'll see all of you in a little while," he said.

Maura started to go, but then turned and kissed Autumn's forehead before leaving. "Love you, sweetie," she said.

"Love you, GiGi."

Hannah watched Bo and Maura walk across the square toward Diane Marsh's shop and noticed that they never stopped chatting, with her father holding up the camera occasionally and both of their heads tilted together as they looked at its gadgets. "Looks like we aren't the only ones who are having a good day," she said.

Matt sat on the floor beside Hannah and looked toward the window, where they could see Bo opening the door for Maura to enter the craft store.

"I kept thinking that she looked a little different today, and I thought it was because of Autumn's story time," Hannah said. "But I'm thinking there's more to it than that."

He nodded. "I believe my mother-in-law may be trying to impress someone."

Hannah thought of Maura's pretty outfit and smiled. Maybe her cheery selection had been made with Hannah's father in mind. "Well, I'm happy for both of them."

"Happy for who?" Autumn asked.

"Mr. Bo and GiGi," Matt answered. "We're glad they're having fun."

"Me, too," she said, grinning. "GiGi is very happy today."

"We all are," Matt said, smiling at Hannah. "Very happy." He looked at Autumn, absorbed in arranging tiny flowers in one of the beds around the faux oak trees. "What doctor are you supposed to call?" he asked quietly.

Hannah should have known he'd ask. "It's nothing to worry about. I had my three month cancer screening last Thursday and am waiting for the results."

"Do they normally take this long to give you the results?" His voice had altered a bit to what Hannah suspected was his doctor-to-patient tone. Soothing, yet depicting concern.

"I usually get them in a couple of days, but I didn't have my appointment until last Thursday. They probably will call before the day is over."

"I could tell your dad's eager to hear that you're okay. Why don't you go ahead and give the doctor a call? Then you can let him know that everything is fine." He smiled. "And I'd like to hear that everything is fine, too."

"You're right," Hannah said, fishing her phone out of her jeans pocket. She dialed the doctor's office.

"Dr. Patterson's after-hours answering service," the voice on the other end said.

"After hours?" Hannah questioned. "I thought Dr. Patterson's office stayed open until 5:00."

"They close at noon on Wednesdays, ma'am, but they will be back in tomorrow morning at 9:00. Is this an emergency?"

"No," Hannah said. "No emergency. I'll call back in the morning. Thank you." She disconnected the phone and looked at Matt. "They close at half day on Wednesdays."

He nodded. "I know a few doctors who do that. But I want you to call first thing tomorrow morning, okay?"

"Okay."

"And after you call your dad and let him know that everything is okay, I want you to call me and let me know the same thing." He smiled, and she did, too.

"I will."

Throughout the next couple of hours, Matt participated way more than Hannah had ever expected, getting down on the floor and situating the tiny fixtures within the dollhouses, painting, gluing, cutting and accessorizing as though he'd been playing with dollhouses for years. Hannah knew better, of course. He was a typical guy and had probably never touched a dollhouse accessory before this week, but this week had been a special one for sure. First of all, he'd gotten his little girl back, and he wanted to spend as much bonding time as possible with Autumn even if that meant crawling around in a display window and playing with dollhouses. And second of all, he and Hannah had definitely found "something" together, and every time he looked at her now, smiled at her, she could sense that the more they were together, the closer they got. And they hadn't even been on an official date yet.

The folks in Claremont seemed even more captivated with watching the new doctor in town working on the scene in the window, and Hannah ended up with more visitors than ever before throughout the afternoon. Mr. Feazell was thrilled, believing he'd probably have a personal record for customers at First Friday.

After they finished working on the display, they had dinner together, and Hannah was thrilled with how well the group got along. Autumn chatted nonstop with Maura, Bo, Matt and Hannah, all of them laughing and eating and spending time together. Occasionally Matt's eyes found Hannah's, and she could almost sense that he felt the same thing as she, that this was like a real family dinner.

When they started gathering their things to leave for church, Hannah realized that they weren't the only ones thoroughly enjoying the time together. Maura touched Hannah's arm at the door.

"I'd like to do this every week, if that's okay for you. This is good for Autumn, times like this." She smiled at her granddaughter. "It's good for all of us, I think."

"Couldn't agree more," Matt said.

"A home-cooked meal every week before going to church together," Bo said. "Works for me."

Hannah grinned. Life was great, really great, and it only seemed to be getting better. "Definitely works for me, but only if you'll let me bring something to help each week."

Maura put an arm around Hannah as the group walked toward their respective cars. "I'll do better than that. Why don't you come over when you get done working each Wednesday afternoon, and we can cook together?"

Matt gave Maura a smile that said he thought there was more to this request, and Hannah figured he was probably right. Maura was trying to play matchmaker, get Hannah over at their place on a regular basis and while she was at it, show Matt that Hannah could cook too. Even Bo glanced at Hannah and grinned knowingly. In fact, he and Maura looked very pleased, very smug even, at the thought of getting Matt and Hannah together. Well, little did they know, Hannah and Matt had started working on that already, especially earlier today with that kiss.

"So, what do you think? This could be a weekly thing then?" Maura asked again. "And maybe you could teach me how to make those dumplings that were so amazing."

"Sounds like a good idea to me," Matt said, which was all the encouragement Hannah needed to agree.

"Sure," Hannah said, walking down the porch steps with Autumn by her side. "I'd love to."

"Wow, look at that view," Bo said from behind them. They all followed his lead to gaze toward Lookout Mountain, where the sun was beginning to drop. Clouds hovered around the notable mountains, but in spite of those clouds, bright rays of that red-orange globe spread a gorgeous deep golden luminance across the sky. "A perfect view for a perfect day."

"Definitely," Matt said. While Hannah had been looking at the sky, he'd moved to the step behind her and his words brushed against her ear.

"It has been an amazing day," Hannah agreed.

Matt walked her to her car, opened the door and waited for her to climb inside. "We'll be right behind you," he said. "Autumn's looking forward to class."

"I am, too." She smiled as he closed the door then turned toward her purse when she heard her cell phone vibrating inside. She tried to keep her phone handy now at all times, since Jana was so close to labor, but she'd forgotten to take her purse in Matt's house. "Oh, dear," she said, grabbing the phone and seeing that she had a voice mail. Surely Jana would have called their father if she'd gone into labor, but Hannah couldn't recall if she saw him with his phone inside the house either. She glanced up and saw that he was already backing out of Matt's driveway, so she couldn't ask him now. She would just have to listen to this voice mail message before leaving. If her sister was in labor, she'd need to get to the hospital. She tapped her horn and got Matt's attention.

He looked in the rearview mirror of his car, and Autumn twisted in her seat to look toward Hannah.

Hannah held up the phone and one finger to let him know she needed to take a call first.

Matt nodded, and Autumn waved, while Hannah entered her voice mail pass code and listened to the message.

"Ms. Taylor, this is Chelsea, Dr. Patterson's nurse. Dr. Patterson needed me to call you and ask if you can come in tomorrow. If you could be here at 9:00, he'd like to talk to you about your tests from last week. If another time is better, just give us a call, but he'd really like for you to come in tomorrow if possible. We'll see you in the office tomorrow at 9:00. Have a good night."

Hannah disconnected, blinked a few times, then forced a smile at Autumn, still waving and smiling from the backseat. She then backed up her car and started driving toward the church, all the while noticing that brilliant sun and the way it pushed against those dark clouds.

Chapter Ten

"Autumn, why don't you get the fishing poles ready for that game we played Sunday?" Hannah worked hard to keep her voice cheerful. "You'll want to make sure the fish are separated and not clumped together. That'll make it easier for all of you to fish for those apostles."

"Okay!" Grinning, Autumn moved to the blue bucket and started working on retrieving the poles. Since she and Hannah had arrived fifteen minutes early, Autumn was the only student in the classroom right now, and Hannah needed to occupy her attention for a while so she could cope with that telephone message.

Sitting at the classroom table, Hannah attempted to get a grip on what she'd be doing tonight. This was the last lesson on Jesus making fishers of men. The kids had enjoyed the fishing game on Sunday, and they all knew how to play it now, so she'd let them spend a little time with that at the beginning of class. That'd give her longer to prepare for acting normal, as though life should continue business as usual, in spite of the fact that her cancer may have returned. And in spite of the fact that she hadn't said anything about it to Matt when he walked with her into the church. How could she tell him what she feared, which would undoubtedly cause her to fall apart, and then teach these precious little boys and girls without them knowing that something was wrong with their teacher?

She closed her eyes and thought about how happy she'd been just moments before she heard that voice mail. Typically after her screenings, the doctor's office called with a brief message informing her that everything was clear. The only times they'd ever called her back into the office were when Dr. Patterson needed to talk to her in person, tell her the status of her cancer and then schedule treatment.

God, I need You now. Help me to be strong.

"I brought you something."

Hannah opened her eyes to see Nathan, his hands wrapped around a small painted clay pot filled with baby pink roses.

"We were at the store, and I saw it. I told Mom that the pot reminded me of the ribbons that you and Miss Jana always wear, and she said we should buy one for both of you because this is the month for those ribbons." He gave her a toothless grin.

A pink breast cancer ribbon had been painted amid the colorful swirls on the outside of the pot, and the tiny roses were exactly the same shade as that ribbon. "That's right," Hannah said. "This is the month for our ribbons." She gently touched her pin and swallowed past the thickness in her throat. October was National

Breast Cancer Awareness month. What if she learned tomorrow that hers had returned?

God, please, she repeated, *keep me strong.*

"You like them? 'Cause you look like you're gonna cry or something. Momma said you might cry."

"She did?"

"Uh-huh, but she told me that was okay, since they would be happy tears."

Hannah nodded. Obviously, Jessica would think they would be happy tears because of her remission. "Well, it was very sweet of you."

"I gave Miss Jana hers in the lobby. She's really big now, you know, not fat-big but baby-big."

Hannah loved this little boy, and she really loved the fact that somehow, with everything on her mind right now, he made her laugh. "Yes, Nathan, I know." She placed the pretty pot on the table and hugged Nathan. "Thank you."

He hugged her back, then pulled away and grinned. "You're welcome." He looked over toward Autumn, lining up the fishing poles on one of the class tables. She had the poles organized by color and all of the fishing strings stretched out so that the magnets on the end dangled in a row along the edge of the table. "Can I go help Autumn now?"

"Sure."

The two of them worked together for a few minutes to get the game ready to go then Nathan asked, "Miss Hannah, can we start playing it now?"

The twins, Matthew and Daniel, entered at that moment and didn't miss a beat. "Can we play, too?"

they asked, their voices blending with the excited question.

"Of course." Hannah smiled. "All of you can play, and your other friends can too when they get here, until I get ready to start the lesson."

"Cool," Matthew said, heading toward the big blue bucket.

Hannah glanced down at her lesson plan, but the words on the page blurred together, and she gave up. Her eyes were barely hanging on to her tears, and she sure didn't want to set them free.

Nathan left the fishing game and moved to stand by Hannah. "Are you sad, Miss Hannah?"

Hannah wouldn't lie to him. "Yes, Nathan."

"Did my flowers make you sad?"

"No, sweetie."

"Well, when I'm sad, I pray. I ask God to make me happy again, and most of the time, he says yes."

"You know what, I think that's the best advice I've had all day."

"Want me to? I can pray for you, if you want me to," he offered.

Hannah took his small hands in hers. "Nathan, I'd like that very much."

He gave her a single nod then bowed his head. "God, please help Miss Hannah to be happy again, because we all like it when she's happy, and I don't want her to be sad. You don't want her sad either, do you, God? Oh, and God, if it's okay with You, let me be the first one to catch all the fish. In Jesus's name, amen."

Again, Hannah found herself laughing because of Nathan Martin.

Thank you, God, for bringing this precious little boy into my life.

Nathan grinned. "See, you're laughing now." He punched a small fist into the air. "God said yes!" Then he hurried back to the fishing game.

Hannah actually did feel better after Nathan's precious prayer. *Thank You again, God.*

As promised, she let the kids play the game while she gathered her materials for tonight's lesson. Hannah always tried to give them something to do while she talked about the Bible lesson. She found that it actually made them concentrate better if their hands were occupied while their minds soaked in the story. Tonight, she'd brought a bunch of fish pictures. There were photos of live fish, cartoon drawings of fish, some posters from *Finding Nemo* and several Christian fish symbols.

When she was ready to start the Bible story, she called the kids over to the table. Nathan arrived first, holding four plastic fish in the air as he sat down. "God said yes," he announced. "Again."

"He got lucky," Matthew said, snarling.

"Boys, let's be nice," Hannah said and decided she'd give a lesson on that another time. Tonight they were talking about fishing for men, and she wasn't ready to venture off the theme quite yet. "Now, while I talk to you some more about Jesus's four fishermen friends and how he wanted to teach them to be fishers of men, you can draw a fish on the paper in front of you." She pointed to the construction paper she'd placed in the middle of the table. "Choose whatever color of paper you want, and then you can pick one of the fish pictures to draw. Or if you'd rather, you can cut out the picture and glue it on the page. Whatever is most appealing to you."

The twins, Matthew and Daniel, always seemed to select the messiest option, and they ran to grab glue sticks and then hurried back to the table. While Hannah told the story, Nathan selected a *Finding Nemo* poster and drew Marlin and Nemo. Autumn had been the last one to leave the fish game, so she sat at the far end of the table from Hannah, but Hannah noticed she picked a white piece of construction paper and a pink crayon to use for her picture.

Hannah told the lesson as she had several times over the past few weeks. The good thing about repeating the story was that the theme was reinforced, and also, the kids began to feel a sense of accomplishment at knowing the characters and knowing their story. Tonight, Hannah would barely get three words out of her mouth before one of them—usually Nathan—finished her sentence with the next part of the story. Occasionally though, Autumn chimed in and gave him a run for his money.

Hannah loved it, and she found herself smiling, really smiling, at the adorable children. After class, the parents came one by one to pick up their children, and Matt stayed behind with Autumn until all of the other children were gone.

"Thought you might want a little help cleaning up again." He grinned, stepped a little closer. "You know, I'm not sure if anyone's ever told you this before, but when a guy spends the afternoon crawling around on the floor playing dollhouses with you and then spends the evening cleaning up messy glue sticks and crayons for you, it might mean something serious."

She smiled. "Oh, really."

He picked up a glue stick that looked like the end had been chewed off and grimaced. "Yep, really."

Matt continued teasing her, and Hannah relished the fun. She needed this, especially tonight, needed something to get her mind off tomorrow, even if only for a little while. Eventually, he looked toward Autumn, who'd remained at her seat and was turning her paper one way and then the other. She smiled, obviously pleased with her artwork.

"She loves this class," he said.

"So do I. I've got to tell you, these kids are therapy for me, one of the best parts of my week."

"Miss Hannah, Daddy, look at this," Autumn said, still admiring her coloring page.

Hannah and Matt moved to the other end of the table. "What did you draw?" Hannah asked.

Autumn had pulled the paper to her chest. "I almost picked the *Finding Nemo* one, since that's my favorite movie, but then I saw that one and changed my mind."

They looked at the picture she indicated, one of the Christian fish symbols.

Autumn smiled and placed the page on the table. The construction paper was bright white, and the fish in the middle was an almost exact replica of the one on the example page Hannah had provided, except the one on that page was in black marker, and Autumn's was in pink crayon.

"Very nice," Matt said. "You did a great job."

"Yes, you did," Hannah said, leaning down to give

Autumn a hug. "I'm proud of how well you do in class."

"Thanks," Autumn said, blushing a little. "But this is the neat part." She had the fish on its side, like the one she was looking at, and she turned the page so it stood upright. "Now look, my Jesus fish is Mommy's ribbon." She pointed to Hannah's pin. "And yours."

Hannah swallowed, breathed in, let it out. "Autumn, you're exactly right."

"Yes, you are," Matt added. "That's beautiful, honey."

"Can we hang it up?"

"Sure," Hannah said, taking the paper. She had a bulletin board on one side of the class for displaying their artwork, and she placed Autumn's fish—or ribbon—in the center.

"Now every time we look at it, we can remember that Mommy is in Heaven, with Jesus. And we can thank God that you're all better now."

Hannah managed to nod, but couldn't control the tears that surfaced with Autumn's words. Luckily, Autumn was so busy admiring her artwork that she didn't notice. Matt, however, touched her cheek and brushed a tear away.

"Hey, you all missed the entire ending of church. You must have had quite an eventful class time." Maura's voice broke through the silence in the room and caused Autumn to hurry toward the doorway.

"Come here, GiGi. I'll show you what I did in class tonight."

Maura followed her granddaughter to the hanging pictures and marveled at Autumn's talent, then Hannah heard the moment that the lady realized what Autumn had really drawn.

"Like Mommy's ribbon, and Miss Hannah's, too," Autumn said, and Maura's hand moved to her throat.

"Oh, Autumn, it's beautiful," Maura said.

"Maura," Matt said, while Hannah turned toward the opposite side of the classroom to get a tissue. She dabbed her eyes and hoped Autumn didn't notice. "Why don't you walk Autumn on out to the car. I want to talk to Hannah a second. We'll be out soon."

Hannah didn't turn around but heard Maura say, "Oh, yes, sure." Her tone said that she also sensed something was wrong with Hannah.

Autumn chatted with Maura as they left, so Hannah knew the moment she and Matt were alone. And when Matt's arms gently wrapped around her, Hannah couldn't hold it in anymore. A soft gasp escaped with her tears.

"Hannah, talk to me. What happened after we left the house tonight?"

She swallowed, brushed tears away, but couldn't speak, couldn't find the courage to tell him. Being a doctor, especially a doctor who had been one of the best research analysts in the nation for breast cancer, he would know what that call back meant. He would know, and when Hannah heard him say it, or saw it in his eyes, it would be official. She'd have no room to think there was any other reason that Dr. Patterson would call her back in tomorrow.

So she didn't speak.

"It's okay. If you don't want to talk about it, that's okay. We can wait." He turned her toward him and pressed her head against his chest. "We'll talk when you're ready, and I promise, I will try to help. Maybe tomorrow afternoon we could take a little time to sit at the square and you can tell me…"

"No," Hannah whispered. Tomorrow afternoon would be too late. She didn't want to know for certain when she told him. She still wanted—needed—to have a whisper of hope. "I need to tell you now."

"Okay," he said, his hand rubbing against her back as he held her, comforted her.

Hannah worked up her courage and finally spoke. "After we finished dinner, I got a voice mail message."

"From—"

"From Dr. Patterson's office. My oncologist. They normally call with the results from my screenings, and usually leave a message saying everything is okay. But when the nurse left the message tonight she didn't provide the results. She just asked me to come in tomorrow so I could talk to Dr. Patterson." Hannah actually felt the tension in his arms as he held her, sensed the beating of his heart growing harder, stronger against her ear. "They always leave the results, you know," she said, then whispered against his shirt, "so I won't worry."

He swallowed thickly, and she felt the pulse of that movement against her forehead. She could sense everything about his emotions right now and what he'd realized too, but she didn't want to see it in his eyes. Not yet.

"The only time they do that is when the news isn't good," she continued, then paused, waited. "Right?"

His heart thundered now, and Hannah didn't know

if she could handle it if he walked away, if he said this wasn't what he had bargained for in this very early stage of their relationship.

Finally, after what seemed like forever, he cleared his throat. "They may have had some substandard readings and so they want to run the tests again."

"But then she'd have said that in the message, wouldn't she?" Hannah asked.

"I'm not sure," he said, but Hannah shook her head, wiped away another round of tears and leaned back to look into those heartrending blue eyes, which were also barely containing his tears.

"I'm afraid, Matt. I'm afraid it's back."

He cupped her face in his hands, tenderly kissed her forehead and then pulled her back into his embrace. "It's going to be okay," he said. "It will. It's going to be okay."

But Hannah wasn't certain if his words were intended only for her, or also for himself. Matt Graham had left a promising career because of what this disease had done to his family, had lost a wife and hadn't been able to communicate with his daughter for two years... because of this disease. And now that he and Hannah were growing closer, it looked like he was getting hit with it again. Hannah swallowed hard. She couldn't do that to him. If her cancer had returned, then she wouldn't—couldn't—put him through all of that again.

God, please, let his words be true. Let everything be okay. Let me be okay.

Chapter Eleven

Matt had never had a more difficult time concentrating at work. Being a doctor meant closing everything else out when you were meeting with a patient, putting that patient's needs above everything else going on in your world. But today, while he moved from patient to patient, he found himself wondering whether Hannah was also sitting in an exam room right now, getting news from her oncologist that could change her life—change their lives—forever. He'd asked her to let him drive her to Birmingham for the appointment, but she hadn't been willing to let him move his own patients around to allow him to leave town. That was the thing about being in his own practice; if he was gone, there wasn't another doctor in his office to handle his patients.

But Matt thought there was more to her request for him to stay in Claremont and for her father and sister to take her to the appointment. Even when they'd left the church building last night and he walked her to her car, he could sense her trying to shut him out.

He had an hour break for lunch, and he walked to his office and dropped into his chair.

"Dr. Graham, I'm going out to grab something to eat. Do you want me to pick up something for you?" Evelyn Gabriel, his office assistant, stood at the doorway and looked at him with a sad smile. She was an elderly woman who had been a medical office assistant in her youth and had wanted to come out of retirement when she saw his ad in the *Claremont News.* Having Evelyn around was like having a grandmother watching over him and his patients each day, and Matt knew she'd detected that he was worried today. She knew he always brought lunch from home, so she was merely checking in on him now.

"I don't want anything, but thanks, Evelyn," he said.

She frowned. "You are going to eat something, aren't you?"

"I don't think so," he said. "But Maura did pack leftovers from last night if I do get hungry."

"Something wrong with Autumn?"

Matt didn't blame her for being concerned. And he knew better than to think she was being nosy; Evelyn asked because she cared. "Autumn's doing great."

"Maura?"

"She's fine."

"Hannah?"

He decided to tell her the truth. He needed to talk to someone, and he hadn't been able to get it off his mind all day. "Hannah got a call from her oncologist last night asking her to come in this morning. She had her cancer screening last week, and evidently this is something to do with that."

Evelyn nodded, understanding evident on her face. "I'll pray for her."

"Thank you."

"And for you."

"Thank you, Evelyn."

She nodded, turned and left his office. Between patients, Matt had tried throughout the morning to reach Hannah on her cell phone, but it went straight to voice mail each time. She'd met with the doctor at 9:00, and it was now noon. Surely she knew something by now.

He fished his phone out of his pocket and dialed again. The phone rang once, twice, three times, and then the line clicked, and Matt heard Hannah sniff.

"Hannah?" he asked. "Hannah, honey, please talk to me. What did he say?"

"It's back," she whispered.

Matt had known that was probably what she'd hear, had known the minute she said the doctor had called her to come in that more than likely her cancer had returned. But hearing it confirmed sent a sick feeling flooding through him and forced his eyes shut. Images of Rebecca when she learned she had cancer filled his mind. And new images, images of Hannah, his beautiful, happy Hannah with her eyes filled with tears, the way they had been last night in her classroom, caused tears to slip from Matt's eyes.

"I start treatments Monday," she said, then sucked in a heartrending gasp that tore at Matt's heart.

"I'll go with you," he said, glad that his tone held strength, when inside he was experiencing the worst pain of his life…again. He couldn't lose Hannah, too. *God, don't let me lose her, please. We're just getting started.*

He knew Hannah was still on the line. He could hear the muted voices of Bo and Jana in the background, both of them sounding distressed. And he was fairly certain he could hear Jana crying.

But Hannah didn't say a thing.

"Hannah, I'll be with you, every step of the way. And it'll be okay." He wanted to know specifics. Where was the cancer and what stage, but he didn't want to ask her now. Now wasn't the time. She needed to cope with receiving the prognosis first, and truthfully, he needed to cope with being in love with another woman with breast cancer. Because even though he hadn't known her long, and even though he certainly hadn't admitted it to Hannah yet, he loved her. Truly loved her. And he couldn't stand the thought of her hurting, of anything happening to her. "I should have gone today."

"I asked you not to," she whispered. "And I wouldn't have wanted to do that to you, put you through this again." Her words trembled through the line. "Matt, I can't do this to you. I have no idea what is going to happen, but I do know one thing. Rebecca's death nearly killed you, and I'm not going to make you go through that again." She sobbed. "I won't."

"Hannah, I want to be with you. I want to help you," he said. "When you get back into town…" he started, but she interrupted.

"No, Matt. I can't. I'm sorry. I care too much for you, care too much for Autumn, to put you through it all again."

"Hannah, listen to me, honey," he said, but the line went dead.

* * *

Hannah asked her father to call Mr. Feazell. She'd finished the display and had just planned to tweak it a bit today and tomorrow morning before First Friday, but there was nothing that had to be done. In all appearances, the display was already an exact replica of the town square, right down to the geese, so she felt okay with calling her work complete. Plus she knew if she went to the toy store, Matt would come, and she couldn't bear to see him yet.

Hannah sat in the passenger seat, Jana sat in the back, and their father drove home from Birmingham. They'd both listened to her conversation with Matt, and then her father had called Mr. Feazell like she'd requested and let him know that Hannah wouldn't be back to the toy store, not today, not tomorrow and not even for First Friday.

"Yes, Ted," her father said. "She's had a rough morning." A pause. "Uh-huh, that's right." Another pause, a grunting sound that said her father was attempting to regain control, and then another, "Yes, but she says the display is good to go, so you're good." He passed a car, and Hannah suspected they were speeding, something her father never did. Then again, he probably didn't have his mind on the speedometer. "Oh, I know that isn't what you're worried about," her father continued. "And yes, I'll let her know." He disconnected, waited a moment then said, "He wanted me to tell you he's praying for you."

"You could have told him the details, Daddy. It's okay. It's in my lymph nodes, six weeks of radiation.

And then we'll see," her voice trailed off to a whisper, "then we'll see how everything went."

Her father cleared his throat and Jana sniffed loudly.

"Jana, honey, please try to stay calm. I sure don't want baby Dee coming before she's ready to get here," their father said.

"I know," Jana whispered from the backseat.

"And sweetie," he said to Hannah, "everything's going to be okay. I really believe that."

Hannah couldn't believe her ears. Her father had spent the last decade primarily angry about her mother's death, about Jana's cancer and then Hannah's. And now he had spent his morning hearing that his youngest daughter's cancer had returned, which was exactly what he'd said he couldn't bear just last week. "You think it's going to be—okay?" Her voice broke on the last word, but she couldn't control the emotion seeping through her tone. "Do you, Daddy? Really?"

Hannah could count the number of times she'd seen her father cry. The first had been the day her mother died. The second at her funeral. Then twice more, when they received the news that Jana had cancer and then that Hannah did as well. So right now, as a thick tear slid down his cheek, made number five. And every time hurt Hannah to the core. Bo Taylor was a strong man and to see him falling apart, to know that she was the reason for that tear, upset Hannah almost as much as the news she'd received this morning.

"Yes, I do," he finally said. "I do believe that everything will be okay this time."

"I do, too," Jana said from the backseat. "Because we're going to pray, and we're going to ask everyone else at church to pray, and we'll do what the doctors say, and everything will be okay."

"We prayed for Mama," Hannah whispered.

"And it was her time to go," Jana said softly. "But I don't believe it's your time, not yet."

Their father wiped at his cheeks. "Neither do I. And we are going to pray. We're going to pray nonstop, and we're going to get everyone we know to pray, just like your sister said. God can heal you, Hannah, and I believe that He will."

Hannah rubbed her own tears away, leaned her head back on the seat and closed her eyes. And suddenly she felt it, too. That feeling that God was in control and that she simply had to let Him take control. If it was His will, then the treatments would work, and she'd truly be cancer-free. And if it was His will that she join her mother in Heaven, then she'd have to understand.

Growing up, Hannah had often noticed a verse that her mother had on a refrigerator magnet. Even after her mother passed, her father left the magnet on the fridge. She believed it was still there, and right now, the verse on that magnet pierced Hannah's thoughts.

"Our God is in Heaven; He does whatever pleases Him." Psalm 115:3.

Hannah closed her eyes, concentrated on that verse, and prayed, "God, if it pleases You, let me be whole again. And if it isn't meant for me to be cancer-free, help me, dear Lord, to be strong enough to handle it."

Jana sniffed again. "Hannah, I know Matt wants to be a part of—" she started, but Hannah stopped her by shaking her head.

"I can't do that to him, Jana. I won't. He lost his

wife. Autumn lost her mother. They basically watched her die while they prayed for her to survive. You didn't see her book from story time last week. Losing her mother affected her so deeply that she stopped talking and felt like her mother's death was all her fault. Can you imagine if she had to go through that again? I mean, just in case—in case things don't get better for me—well, I won't do that to him."

"That man loves you," her father whispered. "I know it, and I think you know it, too. And believe me that there's nothing worse for a man to do than know the woman he loves is in pain."

"If he loves me," Hannah whispered, and in her heart, she also knew it was true, "then that's exactly why I can't put him through this."

Chapter Twelve

"I baked cinnamon rolls," Jana said Friday morning, her happy tone defying the dark circles under her eyes that told Hannah she hadn't slept much, either. "They're your favorite. And coffee, two sugars and lots of cream." She waddled into the living room, where Hannah had kind of slept on the couch all night. "You should have gone to the guest room, you know."

"I never officially went to sleep," Hannah admitted. "Spent the majority of the night watching infomercials and reruns of *Criminal Minds*." The infomercials hadn't done much to take her mind off of her situation, but the crime show had spooked her enough that she actually had a few hours where she was more focused on who the bad guy was than why her cancer had returned.

"You need to sleep," Jana said, placing a breakfast tray on the coffee table in front of Hannah.

"So do you." Hannah hadn't eaten dinner last night, and the cinnamon and sugar drifting through the air reminded her of that fact. Her stomach growled loudly.

Jana managed a smile. "See, eat."

Hannah tossed her heavy afghan aside and reached for the tray. "You're the one that's about to have a baby. I should be ashamed letting you serve me. It should be the other way around."

"Trust me, when she gets here, I'll let you take care of me all you want," Jana said, sitting in the recliner and rubbing her large stomach.

"I'm sorry you didn't sleep well," Hannah said. "I can tell from your eyes, and I know that it's my fault."

"Nope," Jana said. "As much as I love this little angel, I've got to admit that she isn't my favorite person at night right now. Seems that's her favorite time to dance, and most of the time she's dancing on my bladder. You just wait, you'll see…" Her voice trailed off, and Hannah found herself having a difficult time swallowing the bite of cinnamon roll.

Hannah reached for the mug of coffee and took a sip. "It's okay," she finally said. "Even if—" have mercy, this was difficult "—even if I never have children of my own, I'll still get to spend time with little Dee. Surely I'll be able to do that."

Jana scooted forward in the recliner, reached for Hannah's cinnamon roll and ripped off a big hunk. "You are going to have children. You are. I just shouldn't have brought it up right now. It isn't the time to think about it. We've got to get you well first, and then you can get married, have children, have everything you ever wanted. I believe that, Hannah. I really do."

Hannah nodded, ate another bite of cinnamon roll. She wanted to believe it, too. "Five days a week for six weeks. That's how long I'll do the radiation," she said, ready to change the subject and finding that she might as well talk about the main thing on her mind. "Dr. Patterson said it'll probably cause skin irritation, nausea and fatigue, like before. Last time, I had a hard time keeping food down, remember?" she asked, forcing a smile, and then popping another bite of cinnamon roll in her mouth. "So I should enjoy this while I can, right?"

Jana bobbed her head, but her attempts to blink past her tears failed, and her cheeks were instantly coated with shiny paths.

Hannah didn't have the heart to continue, because Jana knew as well as she did that when the six weeks of radiation ended, she'd start chemo, which took all of those potential side effects and added about twenty more. Hannah had the fact sheet for side effects in her purse, but she sure didn't want to look at it again. She'd figure out which side effects to worry about when she actually had them.

By Friday afternoon, Jana had succumbed to the need for a nap and Hannah was working her way through a day of Lifetime movies that had her crying almost as much as her current dilemma. She'd turned off her cell phone in an effort to keep Matt from calling her until she could talk without crying. But when a knock sounded at Jana's door that afternoon, she figured he may have decided for a more direct approach.

Mitch had gone to work at his insurance office and Jana hadn't made a sound from her bedroom since she'd gone back for her nap, so Hannah was on her own to handle whoever was on the other side of that door.

She eased down on the couch and pulled the afghan over her head.

God, let him go away. I can't talk to him right now. I know he loves me, and what's more, I know I love him. And You know I can't hurt him that way again.

The knocking stopped, and Hannah lowered the afghan.

"Thank you, God," she whispered, and then the knocking promptly started again. Hannah tossed the afghan aside and glanced up. "Sometimes You say no, and sometimes You say yes," she said, and walked to the door.

She rose on her toes to look through the top glass of the door and saw that it wasn't Matt Graham on the other side. Opening the door, she found her father and Maura waiting patiently.

"Hey, honey," he said. "We wanted to come by and check on you."

Hannah stepped aside and let them come in. "Thanks," she managed. "But I'm going to warn you, I haven't slept, and I haven't showered."

Maura gave her a tender smile. "We don't care about any of that," she said, then amended, "Well, not about the showering part. You do need your rest, you know."

"I know," Hannah admitted. "But I just can't."

Her father nodded. "Didn't sleep much myself last night, but I've been talking to God about everything all day, and I feel much better." He smiled. "He's in control, Hannah. I really believe it."

Hannah couldn't speak, so she nodded and dropped back onto the sofa. She grabbed Jana's thick gold afghan and again covered up.

For a few moments, they all simply sat in the room, while yet another Lifetime movie played on the television.

"That's a good one," Maura finally said, indicating the movie. "I've seen it a couple of times."

"Me, too," Hannah admitted.

"I've never really watched a lot of Lifetime," her father admitted, "but I may give it a try. I never thought I'd want to scrapbook or go ballroom dancing either, but lots of things have been changing lately. You never know."

"Ballroom dancing?" Hannah asked.

"Maura and I just signed up for the next course over at Stockville Community College," her father said. "I'm kind of excited about it."

For the first time all day, Hannah smiled. "Daddy, I'm so happy for you."

"Me, too," he said, grinning at Maura.

Maura returned the gesture, then turned her attention to Hannah. "He misses you, you know," she said.

Hannah had known the subject of Matt would come up. She'd been merely waiting for it to happen. "I can't talk to him yet. And I can't let Matt go through all of this with me. He's been through it before, and he doesn't need that again. I could tell when I told him Wednesday night about the doctor's call that he was scared."

"He wants to be here for you," she said. "And he's been trying to reach you all day."

Hannah knew that. He'd tried six times since last night before she turned off her phone. "I'll talk to him again, but not yet." She was smart enough to know that in a town as small as Claremont, she couldn't avoid him forever. Plus, there was church, and there was Autumn. No way could she abandon Autumn now, though she had no idea how she could be close to Autumn without hurting her if everything didn't go well.

"Well, when you feel you can, I want you to talk to him," Bo said, standing and moving toward Hannah to kiss her cheek. "I know he's dying right now, not being with you. Think of that, princess. I honestly believe this will hurt him more, keeping him away. Promise me that you'll at least consider letting him be there with you through this. I know he wants to."

"Say you'll think about it, Hannah," Maura coaxed. "Please, for Matt and for Autumn."

"I will," Hannah promised, and she wasn't lying. She'd been thinking about him, and about the two of them together, nonstop. Or more accurately, she'd been thinking about the two of them *not* together nonstop. And it was killing her too.

Finally, Bo and Maura left, and then Jana and Mitch got ready to go to First Friday.

"You sure you don't want to go with us?" Jana asked, as they stood at the door to leave. "I mean, the main reason we're going is to see your display. It was featured in today's paper, you know, and Mr. Feazell promised to turn on *his* town square lights at 7:00." She smiled. "It's a big deal, Hannah, and the whole town is expecting to see you there."

Hannah hadn't even looked at the paper. She glanced at the clock. "It's only 6:00."

"Which means we have time to wait for you if you

want to come!" Jana smiled again, her dimples deep in her cheeks.

"Come on, Hannah. We really don't want to leave you here," Mitch added. "And Jana wants you there, and you know how cranky pregnant women get if they don't get their way."

Jana promptly elbowed him, and he laughed.

"Seriously, we want you to come," Mitch said.

"I really appreciate what you're doing, but I can't go. Not tonight. Take some pictures for me."

Jana withdrew a small camera from her purse. "I will, but I'm sure Daddy will be taking more. He's so excited about this new scrapbooking class."

Hannah nodded, and suddenly wondered if her father would take photos of her over the next few months throughout treatment. When she got skinnier. And bald. And pale. Her eyes watered. "I'll stay here, but thanks. Really."

They left, and Hannah grabbed the afghan, covered up and settled in for what she suspected would be a long, sad night. But before she could relax, there was another knock at the door. She tossed the afghan aside and got up, wondering if Jana had forgotten her key.

"Did you leave something?" she asked, opening the door and expecting to find her sister on the other side.

Matt stood there, tall and handsome, wearing a bright blue button-down shirt that caused his eyes to look even bluer, khaki pants, and an easy smile. "Don't close the door on me," he requested.

She swallowed, blinked past the tears. "I wouldn't do that."

"And don't shut me out, Hannah," he continued.

She couldn't answer to that one, and his smile faded a bit.

"Will you at least hear me out?" he asked, then indicated the wrought iron bench beside the door.

Hannah followed his gaze and saw a shiny red package with a sparkly silver bow balanced on the bench. "What is that?"

His smile returned full force. "A gift."

She couldn't hold back her own grin or the thrill of simply being this close to him again. She'd missed him terribly. "A gift for what?"

"For you," he said. "You can open it out here, I guess, but you may want me to come inside if you don't want all of the neighbors to see you in your pajamas."

Hannah gasped. She'd completely forgotten that she hadn't even gotten dressed today, hadn't showered, and wasn't wearing even an ounce of makeup. And she wore her favorite nearly-worn-out, just-for-comfort flannel pajamas. "Oh, no!"

"You look adorable," he said. "But I thought you might not want everyone to see you looking so…cute."

She did not look adorable. She looked horrendous. And he was standing there, all drop-dead gorgeous and looking at her…as though she were the most beautiful woman in the world.

The tears were uncontrollable.

He leaned over, picked up the package then eased toward the door. "Let me come in, Hannah. And please don't cry."

She sniffed, brushed her tears away. "I can't do this

to you. I'm about to start treatments. I don't want you to have to see that, to have to deal with it all again."

"You aren't asking me to do anything. If you shut me out, though, and keep me from being with you through one of the most important times in your life—" he touched her cheek, wiped away a fresh tear "—then that's something I can't deal with, and it would, quite honestly, tear me apart. It already is. Let me in, Hannah. Please."

"I might not get better. I might get worse. I might— I might—"

"Hannah, I am going to be with you, and we are going to do everything we can for you to get better. I will be with you, praying with you and praying for you, and loving you with everything I've got every step of the way. And to be truthful about it, there's not much you can do to stop that, so you might as well cooperate."

She looked into those beautiful eyes, filled with compassion and undeniably, most definitely, with love. "You said you would be praying with me, praying for me, and..."

"And loving you. I love you, Hannah Taylor. I'd planned to tell you tonight on our date, but you've kind of forced my hand." He smiled, eased toward her and kissed her, slowly, tenderly. Hannah melted against him, absorbing his caress, his compassion, his strength. How did she think she could survive any of this without him? He was her rock now, and she didn't want to be anywhere but right here, in his arms. He ended the kiss, leaned back and smiled again.

"Now's the time where you tell me you love me too."

She laughed. "I do. Oh, Matt, I truly do."

"Wonderful," he said, picking her up and swinging her around on the front porch. When he finally stopped, and Hannah was giggling uncontrollably, he asked, "So, do you think we could actually go in the house now? I think we might be creating a bit of a scene." Then, to Hannah's absolute astonishment, he waved to the neighbors across the street who had apparently watched the entire scene from their front porch swing.

"Hello, Hannah!" Annette Tingle called. "Good to see you're feeling better!"

Hannah laughed again. "Thanks!" she yelled back then she and Matt went inside and closed the door.

"Okay, we spent a little longer talking than I'd planned, but that's all right since they said they would wait for you." Matt tapped the gift box and smiled.

"Since who said they'd wait for me?"

"Mr. Feazell and Autumn. They're not going to turn on the lights to the toy store display until you get there."

She shot a look at the clock. "It's 6:30, and the lights are supposed to be turned on at 7:00. That's what Jana said."

"Yep, it was in the paper and everything. So you don't have a lot of time to waste. But like I said, they'll wait on you. The thing is, I'm afraid kids will be disappointed if we're not there pretty close to 7:00. How fast can you get ready?"

"I haven't even showered."

"Kind of figured that," he said, raising his brows at her PJs. "So, now's the time I learn how long you'll keep a man—and every kid in Claremont—waiting for a woman. Ever heard that Brad Paisley song? It's one of my favorites."

Hannah didn't have time to think of songs right now, though admittedly, she loved that one, too. "Matt, I don't even have anything to wear to First Friday. I only brought sweats and pajamas here. There's no way I can go to the town square in pajamas for First Friday."

He tapped the box. "Never underestimate a doctor being prepared. I got your sizes from Jana, by the way. So take your present and get ready for our first date. You just lost two more minutes."

She threw her arms around him, kissed him thoroughly, the kind of kiss she'd expected would happen tonight during their date. But she felt so close to him, so happy with him now, so *right* with him now. "I love you, Matt. I do. And Jana was right, my dad was right, Maura was right. And you—you're right. I don't want to go through it all without you, but I just didn't want to hurt you again."

"Nothing about being with you will ever hurt me. Being away from you, now that would hurt. That does hurt. I learned that last night and today, and I don't ever want to feel that way again. But we're not going to go that route, are we?"

She laughed. "Doctor's orders?"

"Doctor's orders," he said. "Now go let me see how fast you can get ready. You've lost another minute."

Laughing, she ran from the living room and headed to the guest bath, started the shower and was soon standing beneath the hot water and smiling. Her smile simply wouldn't go away. *God, thank You. Thank You for bringing Matt into my life, and thank You for giving him the strength to go through this with me. He's right, I do want him by my side over the next few months. Thank You, God, for letting me see that Matt wants that too. And please, God, if it be Your will, let me get better. Let us see where our love can go. In Your precious Son's name, amen.*

She finished her shower, dried her hair, put on a little makeup and then opened the shiny package. "Oh, wow." The royal blue cashmere cardigan set was soft and fit her perfectly, as did the sleek charcoal pants. Hannah looked at her reflection in the mirror and noticed that Matt had already added a pink ribbon pin to the top of the sweater. She touched the tiny pin. "Oh, Matt, I do love you." And she smiled, realizing that her mother's last wish for her had now come true.

Only twenty minutes after she'd gone to get ready, she stepped back into the living room and turned around for Matt's review.

"Okay, how do you like it?" she asked.

"You look incredible," he said, "even with bare feet."

She glanced down at her painted pink toes and shrugged. "I think we'll have to run by my place and let me get shoes. I only brought slippers and tennis shoes to Jana's, since I didn't plan to be going anywhere nice. This outfit seems a bit too much for tennis shoes, don't you think?"

He nodded, reached beside Jana's couch and pulled out a smaller, shiny red box. "Which is why I brought this."

"When did you put that there?" she asked, taking the gift and tugging at the silver bow.

"When you were showering. I had it in the car and wanted to give you another surprise." He smiled. "I'm hoping to give you lots of surprises from now on, for as long as you'll let me."

She opened the box and found sparkly gray ballerina slippers, like the silver ones that were her favorites—and Autumn's. "Did Autumn pick these out?"

"She helped," he said.

"Well, they are perfect." She slipped them on, and naturally, they fit just right. "Where is Autumn?"

"Waiting for us at the toy store with Bo, Maura, Jana, Mitch, Mr. Feazell, and I suppose the rest of Claremont."

"So we should leave," Hannah said, looking at the clock. "We actually will only be about five or ten minutes late now."

"Because you didn't leave me waiting on a woman," he said.

"And because you made it easy by picking out my wardrobe," Hannah said, as they walked from the house to his car.

"Okay, I'll confess. I'm something of a shopper. Taking Autumn shopping for clothes is one of my favorite things to do on the weekend. She really likes to dress up, and it makes me happy to make her smile." He opened the passenger door for her then went around and entered the car, while Hannah's jaw dropped.

"You pick out all of those stylish clothes for Autumn? She always looks like she's right off the cover of one of those kid clothes magazines. Picture perfect! I'd assumed it was Maura dressing her so adorably."

"Maura's more an online shopper type. I still like

the old-fashioned method of going to the store, sitting by the dressing room and letting her model things for me, kind of the way you modeled your outfit for me tonight, and then seeing her eyes light up when I buy an outfit she likes, kind of the way your eyes lit up tonight."

"You're amazing," Hannah whispered.

"I'm counting on you always feeling that way," he said, then continued, "Until last week, shopping was one of the few ways I had to kind of communicate with Autumn and know that we were making progress. But now, thanks to you, I don't have to guess what she wants, what she likes. So, in my opinion, you're the one that's amazing."

Hannah felt herself blush. "Well, I have a feeling Autumn won't want to stop those shopping days, just because she's started talking again. That would make any girl feel special."

He paused before turning the key. "Would it make you feel special?"

She smiled. "Of course."

"Then it's decided. Tomorrow's date is a shopping day, just you, me and Autumn, and I plan to watch both of your eyes light up continually."

"That's funny," she said, as he started out of the driveway and toward the town square. "I can't recall you asking me for a date tomorrow."

He nodded, undeterred. "That's right. So I guess I'll go ahead and take care of that now. Every day from now on is a date day, unless you cancel."

She laughed. "That's not even possible."

"Let's try it first and see if it is."

Have mercy, she loved him.

At a few minutes after 7:00, they reached the town square, where cars and trucks lined up solid along both sides of the street for at least three blocks. "Is all of this for First Friday?" Matt asked.

"You haven't been to a First Friday yet?" she asked, surprised.

"Didn't realize it was this big of an event," he admitted.

"Hey, it's a big deal. Everyone in town comes to First Friday. Well, everyone in Claremont goes to just about everything in town. Hey, that's pretty much all we have to do. You should see it when they have the Christmas parade. We'll have to make sure you don't miss that. And Autumn will love it. The floats are incredible and don't even seem like a small-town affair. And the town square is even more crowded, believe it or not."

Groups huddled together as they walked toward the square. Families, teens, elderly couples and church groups filled the streets. Vendors selling cotton candy, balloons and illuminated necklaces were perched at every corner, and a few clowns made their way through the crowds.

"There's a bus. And another one," Matt said. "This *is* really big."

"I told you."

"Yes, but I assumed 'big' by Claremont standards would be quite a bit smaller."

"I'm going to try not to take offense to that, you big-city guy." She pointed toward an asphalt driveway between two parked pickup trucks. "Go through there.

I have a reserved space behind the toy store since I've been working on his display."

"Good thing, since there isn't a single parking space available anywhere near here, and I imagine the majority of the town is waiting for that display lighting."

"It may not be that big a deal," Hannah said. "But I'm flattered that you think so many people would be interested. I'm sure it'll be a good showing and all, but I'm sure they are looking at other things if the display isn't ready yet. Come on, we'll go through the back door." Hannah indicated a small set of stairs leading to a door with a chest and the words *Tiny Tots Treasure Box* painted in the center. "This is it."

Matt followed Hannah through the chaos of boxes in the back storage room and continued through the semi-orderly rows of toys forming the main portion of the store until they spotted Mr. Feazell standing near the display area. He had a hand over his eyes and was searching the street crowd on the other side of the glass. Hannah gasped as they neared. She couldn't see the end of the crowd.

"Are they all waiting to see the display?" she asked, and Mr. Feazell whirled around then sighed with relief.

"Oh, Hannah, Autumn told me you would be here, that Matt was bringing you, but I was starting to get worried. I'm so glad you are here. You've got more people around the store than I've ever seen, and I'm anxious to light the display and let them all come inside and shop! Imagine how many dollhouse kits I'll sell tonight. Sure hope I ordered enough. But maybe if I run out of dollhouses, they'll want the marionettes."

Hannah laughed. "I can't believe how many people are out there."

"Is she here? Is that Miss Hannah?" Autumn eased from behind the display curtain. She had on a navy knit shirt with red trim, blue jeans and short red suede boots.

Hannah glanced at Matt. "You pick that outfit?"

"Of course."

She smiled. "Can't wait till tomorrow."

"They're all waiting, Miss Hannah," Autumn said. "Come on, so I can flip the switch."

Hannah and Matt moved past the curtain barrier so they could stand behind the tiny town square. Hannah immediately noticed that Bo, Maura, Jana, Mitch, Chad, Jessica and Nathan were all on the other side of the glass and clapping with the remainder of the group. Nathan waved wildly when he spotted her through the window, and Hannah waved back.

On Wednesday, Hannah had put the final touches on each dollhouse, making certain every detail was correct on each storefront and then adding real water to the town square's tiered fountain. She also tacked miniature lights along the eaves of the shops and strung them throughout the oak trees that Mr. Feazell had found to place on both sides of the little fountain. The lights added appeal to the display but also made it realistic, since lights actually bordered Claremont's storefronts throughout the year, and since the town covered those big oak trees with lights each month for the First Friday event.

And right now, those lights were what Hannah anticipated would transform the display from pretty to magical.

"Now?" Autumn asked.

Mr. Feazell looked at Hannah, winked and said, "Yes, Autumn. Now!"

Autumn flipped the switch.

Even Hannah was amazed at the beauty of the miniature town square coming to life before the crowd. She'd tested the lighting on Wednesday, but seeing it lit in the day didn't compare to all of the glittering lights at night. The storefronts on the dollhouses reflected the light and the illumination only drew more attention to each tiny detail. Water glistened from the waterfall, and the geese almost looked real, with tiny bits of bread tossed around the ground in front of each bird.

Outside, the crowd cheered and clapped and yelled. And then instantly, they began coming inside, asking where the dollhouse kits were located and which kit was used to make the barbershop, which one to make the candy store, the consignment shop, and so on. Hannah, Autumn, Matt and especially Mr. Feazell were thrilled.

"Thank you, Hannah," he gushed. "It's exactly what you promised!"

After the excitement died down a bit, Hannah told Mr. Feazell that she and Matt were going to take Autumn out to see the children's booths, and he nodded his approval. "Have fun," he said, as he rang up another sale on the old-fashioned cash register. "And Hannah, thanks again. I've never had anything quite like this. It's wonderful!"

"Yes, it is," she agreed, leading Matt and Autumn out of the store.

"Wow," Autumn said, eyeing all of the colorful displays around the square. Bands played at sporadic intervals on the sidewalk, street performers were set up occasionally as well, with some of them dancing, some juggling and some singing. The Sweet Spot had huge candy-shaped decorations covering the entire front of the store, so that it looked like a glowing gingerbread house. "Let's go there!"

Matt grinned. "Sounds great."

They followed Autumn across the square until they ran into Hannah's father and Maura by the Sweet Spot.

"Hey, Daddy," Hannah said, kissing his cheek and then hugging him. "I'm glad to see you here."

"Not nearly as glad as we are to see you here," he said.

Maura looked at her granddaughter and said, "Autumn, would you like GiGi to get you some candy while we're here?"

"Sure!" Autumn took Maura's hand and headed inside, but Hannah's father remained near the entrance with Matt and Hannah.

He stood there for a moment, looking at Hannah, then Matt, and softly smiling. "Everything is going to be great." He looked to Matt. "Did you tell her the news?"

Matt shook his head. "No, but I will."

"He's got it all worked out, honey," he said, pointing to Matt. "And I trust his judgment completely."

"Has all what worked out?" Hannah asked.

"I'll tell you in a little bit," Matt said, kissing her

cheek then wrapping an arm around her while Autumn and Maura exited the candy store with huge swirled candy suckers in each of their hands.

"GiGi said I can go on home with her, if that's okay. She said we're buying a new game at the toy store and then going home to play it."

"That sounds fine," Matt said. He turned to Hannah.

"Coffee?" he asked, pointing to The Grind, Claremont's new specialty coffee shop.

"Sure," she said.

They sat at one of the patio tables and waited for a waitress to take their order. Hannah ordered a white chocolate mocha, and Matt ordered an espresso.

She'd barely sipped her delicious drink but she couldn't wait to find out what her father had been talking about. "Okay, that's as patient as I've got. What news?"

He laughed. "Okay, I get it. You don't keep me waiting long while you get ready, so I shouldn't keep you waiting long when there's something you want to know."

She took another sip of the thick, rich liquid and smiled over the rim of her cup. "Yep, that's pretty much the way it goes."

"Okay. I talked to Bo and Maura today about some calls I made this morning, some arrangements for you, if you want them."

"What kind of arrangements?"

"I called my old research team in Atlanta and asked them to take your case, if you're interested. It'd mean switching doctors, but from what I understand, your oncologist is an affiliate of the research center and should be completely on board with you changing over. If that's what you want."

"And the benefit of changing?" she asked.

"Well, this is going to sound like I'm patting myself on the back, but that research team really is the best in the country at all treatments, traditional and experimental. I'd like for them to take a look at your test results from last week, maybe run a few more tests, and then handle your treatments in Atlanta. I can arrange my schedule so that I can go with you for the treatments."

"They could be daily," Hannah reminded.

"And if they are, I will handle that however I need to. I am kind of the boss of my office, you know."

She'd taken another sip of coffee, and she nearly spit it out when her laugh caught her by surprise. Finally, she swallowed and said, "Yes, I know."

"So," he said, "I kind of made the appointment for Monday afternoon, in case you say yes. And just so you know, I had Bo, Maura, Jana, Mitch, Autumn and myself all praying today and asking God that you would. So basically, I guess I'm asking if you—and God—will say yes."

She took another sip, marveled at how much he'd done for her over the last week. Yes, she'd helped him get his little girl back, but look at what he was doing for her. Giving her the love of her life…and trying to save her life in the process.

Hannah smiled. "Yes. Definitely yes."

Chapter Thirteen

The research center ran additional tests and Matt's old team decided to try a combination of radiation followed by hormone therapy. Hannah completely agreed with their recommendation, not necessarily because she knew whether one treatment was better than another, but because they were Matt's former team, and because he trusted them to do what was best.

And more than merely putting her trust in that team of research analysts and oncologists, Hannah put her trust somewhere else—in God. She prayed, every day, all day. And she knew those around her, those who loved her, prayed too. Bo, Maura, Mitch, Jana, Matt, Autumn, and the entire Claremont community prayed.

By the time that her family and Matt's family gathered together at Jana's house for Christmas, Hannah had completed her treatments and was amazingly feeling very well. She hadn't received the final results yet, but she'd get those in early January, and in her heart, she believed that she'd get good news.

Then again, feeling so well might have been because her life was so unbelievably perfect, with a man that she loved completely, a little girl that she adored, and a family who had supported her through what could have been some of the worst weeks of her life.

Instead, they'd been the best. And this Christmas proved to be one of her best as well, because she had even more family to love. She had Matt, Maura, Autumn…and baby Dee, the beautiful addition that joined the family the day after Thanksgiving and was named after Hannah's mother.

They all ate together, laughed together and then gathered by the tree to exchange gifts. There were several "Baby's First Christmas" gifts for Dee and way more toys than a one-month-old could ever need, which caused everyone to laugh. And Autumn got two dollhouse kits, one from Bo and Maura and one from Hannah, as well as an American Girl doll from Matt. She immediately hugged the doll close, which caused Matt to look at Hannah and mouth a silent "thanks." She'd seen the way Autumn looked at those dolls at the store and had also mentioned to Matt that his pretty little girl reminded her of the American Girl dolls.

Jana and Mitch exchanged silver bracelets engraved with Dee's birth date. Bo and Maura laughed when they opened their gifts from each other; both had purchased craft supplies for their scrapbooking hobby.

When the excitement of the gift opening started to die down, Hannah edged to the tree and withdrew a slim package. She handed it to Matt.

He lifted a brow. "What's this?"

"Open it and see," she teased, sitting beside him on the floor in front of the couch.

"I think it's a tie," Autumn said, which made Hannah smile.

"We'll find out in a second," Hannah said, then tweaked Autumn's nose.

Everyone got quiet to see Matt's gift, and when he pulled the paper away and opened the box, he laughed.

Two long, slender nameplates, one for Matt's desk and one for his door. Both had his entire name and title.

Dr. William Matthew Graham

"No more going incognito for my former profession?" he asked Hannah.

"After everything I've read about you at that research center, all of the news articles and awards I've seen, there's no way you should hide that past." She smiled. "We have a star in town, and I'm proud of him." She reached out and touched her hand to his on the floor. "I'm thinking that he may have saved my life, in lots of ways."

Matt turned his hand so that he could clasp Hannah's. "I love you," he whispered.

"I love you, too."

"And I love you both," Autumn said, scooting toward her daddy and hugging him, then hugging Hannah just as enthusiastically.

Mitch and Jana emitted a combined "Aw."

Maura, who also must have heard their tender declarations, sniffed.

Bo, his arms filled with baby Dee, smiled and said to Matt, "Hey, can you go grab our presents for the girls from under the tree?"

Matt gave Hannah's hand a squeeze. "Sure," he said, then released her hand and moved to the tree to withdraw two thick boxes that were undeniably the size of scrapbooks. He handed one to Jana and the other to Hannah.

"Me first?" Jana asked.

"Sure," Hannah said, and she waited while Jana opened the box and then took her hand to her mouth in awe at the cover of the scrapbook. "Oh, Daddy," she said, and Hannah leaned forward to see that the front of the album was a collage of Jana at all ages, and she saw that many of them contained photos of the entire family, including their mother. "I thought you were doing a track scrapbook."

"Your track stuff is in there," he said. "But once Maura and I got started, well, there was so much that deserved to be featured in a book, so we decided to start from the beginning."

The entire group gathered around Jana and watched the pages play out the story of her life. Baby photos of her trying to eat dirt, then photos of her first skinned knee. Occasional "princess" shots in full dress-up gear, tutu and all. And then, as Jana turned the pages, the entire family photos changed a bit. There were fewer and fewer photos of their mother during the years she was sick, and then they disappeared completely. But there were no photos from the funeral. Instead, Jana's life after, once they actually started living again, filled the remainder of the book. High school track meets, pep rallies before football games, school banquets. Her first date with Mitch. Graduation night. And then the wedding photos. After that, their father had devoted an entire section to pink paper, and these were the photos of Jana going through treatment.

"Because it was a success, and it's something to celebrate," he said.

"Yes, it is," Jana whispered, while Hannah felt the emotion of his words to her heart, and everyone else must have done the same, because the room grew quiet, with only a sniffle every now and then punctuating the silence. She continued through the book until she got to the most recent pictures, the ones of baby Dee. "Daddy, this is the best gift ever."

"Well, it's still in progress, you know," he said, kissing Dee's forehead from where she still slept in his arms. "I'll be continuing with this little girl's accomplishments."

"Or maybe she can have her own book," Autumn said, "like the one GiGi is doing for me."

Bo grinned, winked at Maura. "Well now, I think you're right. Baby Dee should have her own book."

"And he's actually already started it," Maura said, which caused them all to laugh. He'd been taking photos of Dee—and everyone else—all day.

Jana hugged her father then turned to Hannah. "Okay, Sis, your turn now."

Jana, Mitch, Hannah, Matt and Autumn were all seated in the floor, while Bo and Maura sat on the couch. Autumn seemed to enjoy the tight family huddle, and she hopped up on her knees and started clapping as Hannah unwrapped the box, identical to Jana's except with Hannah's name on the tag.

Like Jana's, the front of the album was composed of a collage of Hannah's photos, baby pictures through adulthood. And like Jana's, several of the pictures included their mother. Hannah's eyes were drawn to one in particular, when her mom was serving duty as snow cone mom on the blacktop behind the elementary school. Having your mother as snow cone mom was a big deal, because everyone knew that the snow cone mom always put a couple of extra squirts of flavored syrup on their child's snow cone. Or mixed it with more than three flavors, which was supposed to be the limit. In the picture, Hannah's mother was handing Hannah a snow cone that almost looked tie-dyed it had so many colors, which meant that many flavors. Hannah had begged for a little of everything, and her mother had obliged. And then, as each of the other kids asked for the same, she also gave them the "rainbow" cone. Hannah's friends had dubbed her mother as the coolest, and Hannah had agreed. She still did.

"Daddy," Hannah whispered.

"Snow cone day, huh?" he said. "You know it took her three baths to get the stickiness off her arms, but she never stopped smiling and laughing about all of the fun she had with you and your friends."

Hannah nodded. "I remember."

She turned the page and flowed through memory after memory, her baby photos, little kid pictures, and then right on into junior high and high school. Teeth missing, then reappearing a little bigger.

"Wow, you had really long hair," Autumn said, pointing to a photo of Hannah in her track uniform with a long ponytail dangling well past her shoulder.

"Yes, I did," Hannah said. She'd actually had long hair right up until it fell out with the first round of chemo. Her short hair now didn't have quite the same color as it did back then, and the texture wasn't the same. But she'd gotten used to the short "do" and thought she might even like it better. Matt had mentioned he found her cut sassy and fun, saying it suited her. Hannah hoped her hair would stay throughout all treatments this time. So far, so good.

"It's pretty there," Autumn said, still looking at Hannah's long hair, "but it's pretty now, too."

"Thank you." Hannah continued through the book until she got to the pink section where she was going through treatments.

"We needed to include that, too," her father said softly, "because you're a survivor."

Hannah's throat grew thick. "Thank you, Daddy."

Then she noticed that her pink pages ended and there were red pages at the very back of the book. "Daddy?" she asked, turning the last pink page and finding…Matt.

"Red is for love," Autumn said, and Hannah smiled, gazing at the photos that her dad had been snapping over the past few months.

She and Matt inside the display area at the toy store. Then walking in the square. Feeding the geese. In Hannah's classroom at church with Autumn smiling between them. She flipped the page, and there were more photos, some that her father had applied special photo techniques, antiquing a picture of Matt kissing Hannah's cheek and removing all color from one of the two of them taking turns pushing Autumn on the swing at Hydrangea Park. Their emotions, the happiness of all three of them, seemed further intensified in the black-and-white image, and Hannah touched a finger to Autumn's smile, then Matt's and then her own. "That was a fun day." They were all wearing jackets and scarves, because the photo had been taken in early December, but it was the day after Hannah's last treatment, and she'd wanted to celebrate at the park. Her father and Maura had asked to come along, and now she knew why, so he could take pictures like this. "I love this, Daddy," Hannah said at the last page.

"Well, you aren't done yet," he said, his smile creeping a little higher into his cheeks. "There's one more photo on the back of that one, and it's *my* favorite."

Hannah turned the page and saw Matt kneeling beside Autumn, one arm around her and the other joining her small hands to hold out a small, black box. Hannah blinked, wondering if she was imagining what she saw in that picture, and in that box.

"Hannah," Matt said from behind her.

At some point when Hannah was looking through the photos, Matt and Autumn had edged away from the group, and now they stood together, Autumn's hand over her mouth to control her giggles. Her other hand, like in the photo, joined Matt's to hold the black velvet box in front of them and the ceiling light seemed to spotlight the exquisite marquise cut diamond inside that box.

"You're supposed to say yes," Autumn said.

"But I haven't asked the question yet," Matt said to his little girl.

Autumn's mouth quirked to the side. "Sorry, I forgot that part."

Matt, and everyone else, laughed. "That's okay. But I should probably ask anyway."

"Okay," Autumn said, her giggles still mingled

through her words. She looked at Hannah. "Daddy needs to ask you something."

Matt scooted forward, and since Autumn still held on to one side of the box, she shuffled along. "I asked your father for your hand in marriage," he said, "and in case you're wondering, he said yes."

"And then Daddy asked me if I wanted you and Daddy to get married, and I said yes, too," Autumn said, then she leaned forward and kissed Hannah's cheek. She cupped her hand and whispered, rather loudly, in Hannah's hear. "Now you need to say yes, too." Then she scooted to the side and stood beside Maura.

Matt removed the ring from the box and took her left hand. "Hannah Taylor, I love you, and I want to spend the rest of my life showing you how much."

Hannah was overwhelmed, her heart flooding with love for the man whose eyes looked into hers and were filled with undeniable love. She knew that he hadn't officially asked, but she could barely wait to answer the question.

"Hannah, will you…"

"Yes!" she squealed then jumped forward, her arms wrapping around him and her laughter filling the room. Her momentum was more than she bargained for, though, and they both toppled backward. "Yes, yes, yes!" she continued, while the entire room burst into cheers.

Epilogue

~❧~

Mitch Gillespie wore the same silver tuxedo as the other groomsmen, but he had a unique addition—six-month-old Dee, wearing as much pale pink lace as would fit on her tiny body—nestled in his arms.

"Hey," Mitch said, peeking into Hannah's classroom, where the bridesmaids were gathered and waiting for their cue. "Dee wanted to get an early peek. You know me, I was content to wait, but she wouldn't listen." He grinned. "And she wanted a kiss from Mommy."

Jana laughed and made her way to the door, kissed her daughter and then kissed her husband too.

"You're terrible," Jana said.

"You love me," he reminded, and she giggled.

"Yes, I do."

"Come here, precious," Hannah cooed, moving toward them and reaching for Dee.

"You sure you want to do that?" Mitch asked. "It hasn't been long since she ate, and you know how she is about losing her meals every now and then."

"A little spit-up never hurt anybody," Hannah said.

"Maybe not, but I'm betting most brides don't walk down the aisle with any on their dress," he said.

"You'll hold it all together for Aunt Hannah, won't you, Dee?" Hannah said, scooping the little redhead into her arms. "There ya go."

Dee reached for Hannah's hair and managed to clasp a lock in her fingers.

"Whoa, sweetie," Hannah said, laughing. "Goodness, you're getting strong."

Jana laughed and eased her little angel's hand free of Hannah's hair. "Your hair looks very pretty," she said, "so let's try to keep it that way, at least until you've walked down the aisle. During the reception you can let her destroy it if you want."

"I was so lucky that the treatments didn't make it fall out this time."

"Favor of God, I'd call that," Maura said from behind her, and Hannah nodded.

"Definitely the favor of God." Hannah kissed Dee's cheek and nuzzled those soft red curls. She couldn't wait to hold her own baby one day and to start raising Autumn with Matt now. She adored Autumn and was thrilled that she'd been so excited about the wedding.

"I just love these shoes!" Autumn said, holding up the hem of her pink dress so she could see them in the mirror on the back of Hannah's classroom door.

Hannah smiled. "Well, I knew the minute your daddy asked me to marry him what shoes we had to get. Remember, you told me that you wanted to wear those in a wedding one day," she said.

Autumn giggled. "I said I wanted to wear these kind of shoes when I got married. And that made you laugh," she said, moving the sparkly ballet slippers one way and then another to view them in the mirror.

"Well, I figured you wouldn't mind wearing them in my wedding."

"I sure don't," Autumn said, still smiling.

"Me, either," Jessica Martin said. She stood behind Autumn and was also admiring her sparkly shoes, as well as her pretty pale pink bridesmaid dress.

"Hey, I think I'm up," Mitch said, kissing his wife on the cheek before heading out.

Jana and Jessica followed him, and Hannah waited until the music for the groomsmen and bridesmaids ended, then she sent Autumn out to meet Nathan.

"I drop the flowers by myself, right?" Autumn asked, before heading out. She looked so pretty in the pink lace dress with her dark hair in beautiful long ringlets and sprigs of pink-tinted baby's breath tucked throughout the curls. "Nathan doesn't help?"

"You can let him help if you want," Hannah said, grinning. They were such good friends. "But he will be fine just to hold on to the ring pillow."

"Okay," Autumn said, opening the door. She stopped, and Hannah wondered what had happened. She'd been a pro during rehearsals, knowing exactly when to go, how slow to walk and when her music cue began. "Miss Hannah?"

"Yes, honey?" Hannah moved to the doorway. "What is it, Autumn?" She prayed Autumn wasn't changing her mind about Hannah and Matt marrying. She'd said she was happy and it would break Hannah's heart if she wasn't. "You can tell me, sweetie. Anything at all. You can always talk to me."

"I love Mommy. I always will." Those dark eyes that had been filled with sadness on the day they'd met studied Hannah now.

Hannah's throat clenched. "I know that, honey. I wouldn't want it any other way."

"But I talked to Daddy and he said I'd need to talk to you about something."

"Okay," Hannah said, unconcerned that Autumn's cue had passed and that the pianist seemed to be trying to start the section over. This was more important. "What did you need to talk to me about?"

God, let me handle this right.

"Would it be okay, since you're marrying Daddy today, if from now on…"

"What, sweetie?"

Autumn chewed her lower lip, looked down at her shoes again, and then lifted those dark lashes. "Can I call you Mommy, too?"

Hannah didn't even attempt to stop the tears this time. She scooped the precious little angel into her arms and held her, kissing her forehead, her cheeks and then holding her in an embrace that she prayed conveyed how much Autumn's request touched her heart. "Yes, that would be absolutely fine."

Autumn leaned back, smiled then took her fingers to Hannah's cheeks. "You've got those marks again."

Hannah laughed. "Don't worry. I'll clean off the mascara before I walk down the aisle. And these are happy tears, very, very happy tears, so it's definitely okay."

"I love you," Autumn said.

"I love you, too, sweetie."

Autumn turned, and Hannah heard Nathan yelling at her to hurry, and she was fairly certain she heard the crowd laughing a bit from inside the church, which made her smile.

"She does love you, you know," Maura said from behind Hannah.

"I know. I love her too."

"And in case you're wondering, I'm happy that she feels comfortable calling you Mommy, too. That's exactly what Rebecca would have wanted." Maura moved to Hannah and wrapped an arm around her, gently squeezing her against her side. "This has been such a blessing, that you're cancer-free and now you and Matt are becoming a family, giving Autumn a true family again. God is good indeed."

Hannah smiled. "Yes, He is."

Then she heard her cue, hugged Maura once more and said, "I'll see you in the church."

Maura smiled. "Yes, you will."

Then Hannah met her father in the lobby of the church.

"Well, you ready?" he asked, grinning.

"Absolutely ready."

They stepped through the doors, where from the look of the packed pews the entire town of Claremont filled the auditorium. Everyone stood and smiled at Hannah as they passed and made their way to the front of the auditorium. Jana and Jessica stood for Hannah, Mitch and Chad stood for Matt.

Hannah kissed her father on the cheek before he released her arm and went to stand next to the spot where Matt would be standing shortly.

The guests remained standing, and Hannah turned to see her future husband at the lobby waiting. Then she saw Maura, wearing a pale-pink-and-cream wedding suit, step to his side. A loud sniff to her right caused a look to her father, and his smile touched her all the way to her soul. This was what she had prayed for, all of it, Hannah finding someone who would love her for life, and their father also finding someone who would make his life complete, someone he could love and share his life with. Someone to be a part of him, the same way Hannah would have Matt as a part of her.

She watched as Matt walked Maura down the aisle, and Maura joined Hannah's father, and Matt joined Hannah. Then they turned to Brother Henry who was smiling, and crying.

"This is beautiful," he said, before starting the ceremony. "Undeniably beautiful."

Matt leaned toward Hannah. "Certainly is beautiful, all of this, and you," he whispered. Then, while Brother Henry thumbed through the scriptures and prepared to speak, Matt continued. "Isn't it great when..." he started, then paused and looked to his bride, to the woman that would be his wife today and forever. "You know the rest," he prompted. "Isn't it great when..."

Hannah smiled, suspecting they would do this the rest of their lives, and she completed his tender thought. "When God says yes."

* * * * *

Dear Reader,

Current statistics show one in every eight women in the United States will develop breast cancer over the course of her lifetime. By telling Hannah's story, I tried my best to cover the way she held on to her faith for both the good and the bad news she received from having the disease. Battling trials brings us closer to God, but some choose to turn away from God in times of struggle. I hope that *Healing Autumn's Heart* may cause someone who has turned away in times of struggle to reconsider their faith and hopefully find their way back to our Savior.

I enjoy mixing facts and fiction in my novels, and you'll learn about some of the truths hidden within the story on my website, www.reneeandrews.com. You can enter a contest on my website to win a pair of Toms shoes similar to the ones worn by Hannah in the book. I am very impressed with this company and the fact that they donate a pair of shoes to a child in need for every pair purchased.

Additionally, my website includes alternate scenes for some of my novels and deleted scenes that didn't make the final cut. If you have prayer requests, there's a place to let me know on my site. I will lift your request up to the Lord in prayer. I love to hear from readers, so please write to me at renee@reneeandrews.com.

Blessings in Christ,
Renee Andrews

Questions for Discussion

1. The book begins with Matt's concern over Autumn's silence. He finds himself praying to God, even though he hasn't prayed in years, just in case God might help his child. How hard is it to pray after you've lost touch with God? Was it really all that difficult for Matt to find his way back, and how did Hannah help?

2. Claremont is a town similar to the town I live in, where everyone really does know everyone and cares about each other. How can this be beneficial in living a faithful life? How could it be a hindrance?

3. Hannah's family has at least one weekly dinner together, they go to church together and occasionally have "Family Fun" days together. How do you think family bonding such as this affects the family unit? Do you think families still spend this type of quality time together, or do you feel that it's been tossed to the wayside with the fast pace of modern society? If so, what can we do to put priorities back in order, the way God intended?

4. Nathan Martin had prayed for Autumn before he really even knew the little girl. How important is it to teach children to turn to prayer in times of struggle? How can we emphasize this to our children, so that they turn to prayer first?

5. Hannah's father, Bo Taylor, attends his first church service in over a decade. Have you ever returned to a church after being gone for a while? How hard or easy was it to come back? Did the members welcome you, or did you feel a little bit of resistance at your return? How could you compare the parable of the prodigal son to Bo's return to church?

6. Bo and Maura strike up a friendship that seems to be heading toward something more. How did you feel about this? Were you happy that they'd found a second chance at love, or did you think there was something inappropriate in their relationship? Explain.

7. Some of my favorite memories growing up involved the big gatherings for church fellowship meals. I attempted to describe a similar "dinner on the grounds" in this book. How do you feel church fellowships can help a congregation grow closer? What are other ways of bonding the church can do outside of regular worship meetings to strengthen the relationship between members?

8. After he lost his wife, Matt asked his mother-in-law to move with them to Alabama and to care for Autumn while he was at work. What does this say about Matt? What does it say about Maura?

9. Matt mentions 1 Corinthians 10:13. Read this

verse and define a point in your life where you felt, like Matt, that there was something you just couldn't bear. Did God have you face that trial? If He did, did you grow closer to Him, or did you turn away? What can we do to ensure that we turn to God during those tough times? What can we do to ensure that our children do the same?

10. Toward the end of the story, Hannah gets some unexpected news about the state of her health. Though she thinks Matt will respond a certain way, he acts in a completely opposite manner. Did you think Matt would be as supportive? Why or why not?

INSPIRATIONAL

Inspirational romances to warm your heart & soul.

TITLES AVAILABLE NEXT MONTH

Available October 25, 2011

SLEIGH BELLS FOR DRY CREEK
Return to Dry Creek
Janet Tronstad

THE LONER'S THANKSGIVING WISH
Rocky Mountain Heirs
Roxanne Rustand

CHRISTMAS GIFTS
Gail Gaymer Martin and Brenda Minton

THE FOREST RANGER'S HUSBAND
Leigh Bale

BIG SKY FAMILY
Charlotte Carter

LAKESIDE REUNION
Lisa Jordan

LICNM1011

REQUEST YOUR FREE BOOKS!

2 FREE INSPIRATIONAL NOVELS
PLUS 2
FREE
MYSTERY GIFTS

Love Inspired

LIREG11B

Here's a sneak peek at SNOWFLAKE BRIDE
by Jillian Hart, coming November 2011
from Love Inspired Historical.

"Are you interviewing with my mother this morning?"
Lorenzo asked.

"Yes. Thank you." Ruby plucked the buttons from him
quickly, because she'd made her own mittens and they were
a sad sight. She was only learning to knit, and the uneven
gauge showed.

He didn't seem to notice. "I know she's looking for
someone dependable. Her last kitchen maid eloped with the
neighbor's farmhand without giving notice, so Ma is particularly miffed about that. Mention you are as dependable
as the sun, and she'll hire you."

His advice was nice, but why would he bother? "You're
giving me an advantage."

"Guilty. It would be nice to see a friendly face around the
house. I miss everyone from school. Don't misunderstand
me, I love working on the ranch, but I spend more time with
cows and horses than people." Those dimples deepened and
held her captive.

Surely a sign of impending doom. She could not let a
handsome man's dimples draw her in like that. What was
wrong with her? She tried to hide her smile and stared at
the toes of her shoes. She needed to repair her shoe in time
for her interview. How could she do that while he watched?
Surely, as nice and kind as he was, Lorenzo couldn't help
drawing conclusions.

"Let me drive you up to the house." His warm offer star-
tled her.

"D-drive me?"

"It will give you time to sew everything on. My mother will never suspect." Kindly, he held out his hand, palm up, as an invitation. "You can sew while I drive."

Did his unguarded blue eyes have to be so compelling? Veiled in the snow, he could have been a Western legend come to life, too dreamy to be real and too incredible to be speaking to her.

Don't do it, she thought. Her pa had raised her to be self-reliant. She was perfectly capable of walking the rest of the way. Besides, she was too shy to think of a thing to say to him on the drive. She should simply say no.

"C'mon. I'm not leaving without you. If you walk, I walk."

"I suppose one short little ride won't hurt."

Look for
SNOWFLAKE BRIDE
by Jillian Hart, available November 2011
from Love Inspired Historical.

SHLIHEXP1111

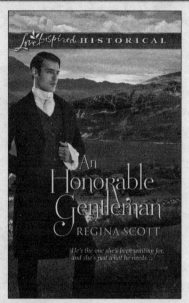

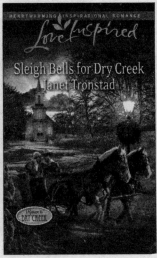